Long Way Home: A World War II Novel

Cheryl A. Head

ISBN 978-1500523947

Library of Congress Control Number 2014912979

Cover Design by Bobbette Rose

CreateSpace Independent Publishing Platform

An Amazon Company

North Charleston, South Carolina

Dedication

PFC Samuel McGarrah (Dad)

PFC Lillian DeVane (Friend)

Thank you for your service!

Acknowledgements

Michele Orwin, who first encouraged and read;

Hurston/Wright Writer's Workshop & Marita Golden

for the discipline and tough love; Furious Flowers

Writing Group; Renee Bess for inspiring; Peggy

O'Brien for acts of friendship; Olivia Steele for the read

and feedback; Leigh Mosley for believing, and Angie

Head for unconditional love.

Cover Photo

World War II at Huachuca, James P. Finley, *Huachuca*

Illustrated Vol. 9, 1993

Part One

July 1943

Chapter 1

(Georgette)

It is nearly dawn, a precious hour for myself before I surrender to the strawberries—full, ripe and ready to be picked. I try a new hair style this morning swept high in a bun the way Lena Horne wears hers in *Stormy Weather*. I lean close to the mirror, and trace a finger along the ridge of my nose and the curve of my mouth. I sort of favor Lena, except I am darker, shorter, and have full lips.

As I grab a bobby pin I catch a glimpse of *The Saturday Evening Post* open to a photograph of six attractive WAVES smiling arm-in-arm in front of a Liberty Ship. They wear crisp white blouses with calf-length white skirts, white pumps and black and gold braiding on their caps. Behind them sailors stand single file on double decks and they all look proud to be serving their country. I can picture myself wearing a WAVE uniform but they won't accept colored girls in the Navy, so I've made up my mind to join the Women's Army Auxiliary Corps. I've shared my plan only with my sister, Barbara, but today I'll tell Boone.

"Yes, WAACs really *are* important to the war effort. They deliver mail, drive ambulances, and serve as clerks. Any job that can free up a man to fight."

Boone isn't convinced. We lean our backs against a post in the fence that separates my father's thirty-acre farm from the neighbor's equal number. Boone's long legs stretch out towards the meadow and mine are tucked under my skirt the way ladies are taught to sit. The grass is soft and smells of dried morning dew. A pecan tree provides shade for us as we finish our noon meal sharing sips of cool lemonade from a Mason jar.

"I saw the pictures in *Life* magazine. One girl was driving a Jeep and some others were marching with guns..."

"Those aren't real guns, Lil. They don't let WAACS shoot." Boone stares at me for a moment. "Besides, I just don't want no girlfriend of mine joining the WAACs."

Boone and I have kept time since the year before I graduated high school and he is considered quite the catch. He's smart, loyal and curious about the world, everything I want in a husband except he is stuck in Pender like me.

Everyone expects me to continue the tradition of generations of women in my family raising kids and crops, but I've known for a long time it's not the life I want. I wish I could make Boone understand that what tugs at my soul night and day is stronger than the things he can offer.

"If you're so set on getting away, why don't you find a job in Wilmington? You're a bright girl and there are lots of jobs for women in the factories. Plus, you'd be close enough that we could see each other every week."

"Boone, I won't be satisfied being just a few hours away. I know there is more to life than North Carolina and this farm and…"

"And me?" he accuses.

I reach for his hand. He pulls me in close and his jeans feel rough against my legs. His lips touch a dozen places on my neck as I sink deeper into the grass. With some effort I push him away. "Boone, you know we can't."

He rolls onto his back and we lay side by side not touching. In our community of multi-generational farms, extended kinships and church families, personal passion is rarely a private matter. Boone and I have made youthful promises to each other that we may or may not keep but our connection to legacy is older than our desire.

The fertile ground cradles us and the sun plays a game of peek-a-boo through the pecan leaves. I rise to gather up the remnants of our food and pack it in my lunch pail. Boone walks me back to the strawberry patch and kisses me again before returning to his own chores. He didn't even notice my new Lena hairdo so I put on my sun hat and adjust it low over my forehead.

In two hours, I fill a dozen large baskets with plump strawberries. The soil is musky and perspiration drizzles down my legs leaving even lines of dust that remind me of the rows and rows of plants surrounding me. In my twenty years I've never set foot out of Pender County and most days the hard work smothers thoughts of escape but today I would leave with the first stranger who offers a ride to a new adventure.

I hear the grind of gears as a vehicle climbs the steep road next to the field and I pause as it comes into view. It is a bus transporting another group of young army recruits.

"Hey sweet thing," one of them shouts. He is a handsome boy with a flash of white teeth against mahogany skin. His muscular arms dangle from the bus window and a half dozen other boys poke out their heads to give him encouragement. I return to picking berries.

"Aw baby, why you gonna do me that way?" the fresh boy hollers, dabbing at fake tears with his cap.

I offer a smile and his buddies howl. I watch the green bus lurch up the road, dust swirling high in the air like a funnel, and disappear into the tall Carolina pine trees. I want to run after it but the earth holds fast to the soles of my boots and the strawberry plants cling to my legs, heavy with the fruit that demands their own release.

My mother is at the stove putting the finishing touches on supper. The farm is my father's domain but she is in complete charge of our domestic order. The kitchen overflows with the good smells of her cooking and I watch as she mixes meat juices with flour to make brown gravy. Finally I get up the nerve to tell her I want to sign up with the WAACS. She shakes her head 'no'.

"I'd only be gone a couple of years and I would write every week. Barbara and Helen are old enough to take over my chores and I could even send a little money home to you and daddy," I plead.

"Sis, you know what they say about girls who join the army. Mrs. Shepherd's girl joined them WAACS, and you know how mannish she is, you're not like that."

"No ma'am," I say in a harsher tone than I intend. "But, I'm not like you and grandma either."

Mama always listens and tries to understand me. She has more than once remarked about what she calls my wanderlust but I can tell this time my words have hurt her. She slides the skillet of gravy off the flame and turns to face me. I am my father's child in temperament—stubborn, impatient and quick to anger but I look like my mother. We share the same almond-shaped eyes and the hollow look she gives me now is the one I see in the mirror each morning. She straightens to her full, five-

foot-four inches and purses her lips the way she does when she
has something important to say.

"I'll talk to your father about it today Sis," she promises.

Then she holds me close, our foreheads pressed together.
"Sometimes the shortest way home, is the long way round," she
whispers.

Our family eats supper in the kitchen at the oak table daddy
built after Helen was born. Daddy is a proud man and the farm,
which has been in his family for decades, is his life's work.
He and mama sit at each end in matching high-back chairs that
have broad arms and an inset of padded burgundy fabric at the
headrest. My sister Barbara and I sit across from the younger
girls, Helen and Ruthie, on sturdy oak benches. Barbara is two
years younger, Helen four years my junior and ten-year-old
Ruthie's legs have just this month grown long enough for her
feet to touch the floor when she sits.

Daddy begins the blessing over our food in his usual way
but instead of ending with 'for the nourishment of our bodies,'
adds: 'and Lord, we thank you for holding our family together
during this time of war.' When I open my eyes he glares at me
so I quickly close them again. We each hand our plates to him
to be served the meal's meat and then we pass side dishes
around the table. Most times our suppers are filled with talk of
my father's day and the state of the world. But tonight there are

no lectures about how money doesn't grow on trees, or the war with Germany, so Ruthie takes it upon herself to pierce the unusual quiet.

"One of the pigs got loose today, daddy, and ran through the front yard. It was Penelope (Ruthie has given names to all the pigs) and we all had to chase her. Then Helen slipped in the mud and messed up her dress and..." Ruthie chatters on all the while separating her food into little mounds on her plate which always agitates my father. She is a picky eater and often gets a lecture from daddy that begins: "how many times have I told you not to play with your food. Food is for eating. There are some people living in Africa who don't even have food because Africa has a famine. You know what that means girl?" Of course Ruthie knows what a famine is, we all do since daddy goes on and on every week about the Africans he's read about in the *National Geographic*. Apparently, it's the only reading material at the barber shop because Boone tells me he also knows about the famine but is more interested in the magazine's pictures of naked African girls.

"Ruthie!" daddy bellows startling all of us, including mama. "Eat your food, and eat it now!"

Poor Ruthie cleans her plate in four, huge gulps of peas mixed with rice mixed with pork and gravy and I'm sure it's a shock to her stomach for all that food to come rolling down together. Supper continues in complete silence. Barbara, Helen and I give Ruthie sympathetic looks but otherwise we watch our own peas, afraid to make eye contact with daddy. I peek at mama several times during the meal looking for a cue that she has kept her promise to speak with my father about joining the WAACS, but there is no eye contact so I decide to take a risk.

"I saw a busload of army recruits this afternoon."

Everyone looks at me but no one responds. Mama begins scooping vanilla pudding into bowls for our dessert and tops each bowl with sliced strawberries.

"How soon before the strawberries are cleared from the east field, Sis?" daddy asks before shoveling a spoonful of pudding in his mouth. He is a large man with skin the color of ripe chestnuts. He has a full beard and licks at his mustache to capture a glob of stray pudding.

"I think a couple more days."

"Good, because if it rains this weekend they will be too wet to pick.

"Yes sir, I'll get it done before then," I say feeling miserable.

Two days have passed and my father still hasn't said a word about me joining the army. It's Saturday and Barbara and I spend the morning helping daddy with the tobacco crop. We pull the yellowing leaves at the bottom of the plants and spear them onto a tree branch which he will later hang from a pole across the rafter of our curing shed. The work requires constant bending and just a few hours causes backache along with numbed fingers from the nicotine. When Barbara and I finish in the field we return to our house to help with the tasks reserved for womenfolk.

Mama has a schedule for the maintenance of our home and Helen and Ruthie are busy at their chores. Each week, furniture in our large, one-story house is dusted, wood floors in the three bedrooms are swept and one set of windows are washed inside and out, this is also the week the mattresses on the beds are turned. Mama is doing laundry and Barbara and I take over so she can prepare supper. It feels wonderful to dip our hands into soapy water after handling the greasy tobacco leaves. The day lingers on in predictable routine.

"Has daddy said anything to you yet about the army, Sis?" Barbara asks.

I consider my sister a friend and I've shared my biggest secrets with her like how I feel about Boone and how I dream of moving away from Pender. But even she was surprised when I divulged my desire to become a WAAC.

"No, but mama has already spoken to him and she says I should just be patient. Why do grown folks put so much stock in patience?"

My question is an expression of my exasperation and doesn't require an answer but Barbara offers one anyway.

"I guess it comes with living on a farm. You learn everything happens in its own time. That's why daddy is always telling you to slow down, Sis."

"Jesus, if things get any slower I'll be dead."

Barbara gasps and looks toward the porch door. "You better not let mama hear you take the lord's name in vain," she warns.

In our family, Barbara doesn't stand out in any way. She's not the oldest, the youngest, nor the prettiest like my sister, Helen. She is a steady girl and will not disappoint my parents. She will remain in Pender and be a dutiful daughter.

"Barb, why can't daddy understand I'm different? I'm young and I want to see something of the world, not just read about it in a magazine."

"But joining the army, Sis, isn't there another way?"

After supper is eaten and the dishes and kitchen cleaned, mama calls me into the living room. Daddy's routine is to retire to his chair, light his pipe and read the paper but this evening he holds the bank deposit book. I look at his hands. His fingernails are almost always dirty. Even when he washes for supper or church his hands never seem to be free of the earth he digs in every day.

"Sis, come and sit down," he orders.

My family nickname is Sis, and Boone calls me 'Lil' but my given name is Georgette Lillian Newton, named after my father. I sit next to mama on the settee, she smiles and covers my hand with hers.

"I remember what your teachers said when you graduated high school," daddy says. "They said you had *potential*."

Daddy mouths the word like it is a disease. He stares at the bank book then looks up at me.

"Well girl, your mama and I have talked it over and we got a little money set aside that we want you to use for that teachers' college in Florence near where your Aunt Shirl lives."

Daddy stops talking and smiles displaying even, white teeth.

My heart sinks. I don't want to go to teachers' college, and I sure don't want to live with my stuffy Aunt. I'm sure my mother has told her only sister about the WAACS and Aunt Shirl has reluctantly agreed to take me in. She wouldn't want tongues wagging about her niece going off to join the army.

The grandfather clock in the corner ticks loudly and the pendulum swings in slow motion. My father waits for my response to his good news but my mother senses my mood and glances nervously at me. She pats my hand rapidly.

"Daddy I know it's a sacrifice to use the family savings to send me to college, and a hardship to lose my help on the farm,"

11

I speak slowly, trying to contain the discontent rising in my chest.

Daddy smiles even broader now.

"But, I don't want to stay with Auntie Shirl. She's nosy and mean, and rarely has a good word to say to or about me. She favors Helen."

My father knows all this is true. He doesn't get along with my aunt either.

"But Shirl told your mama she'd be glad to have you, Sis."

His smile is gone and I know what I say next will end the peace in the room but I don't care. I stand and purse my lips. Mama stands too.

"It's not just Auntie Shirl. I don't mean to disappoint you but I don't want to be a teacher or a farm wife, I want adventure and that's why I'm going to join the WAACS."

My words begin as an appeal for understanding but end as defiance. Mama quickly steps between me and daddy as he moves forward. As short as she is, she still manages to lower the arm he's raised to slap my face.

"Sis, don't dare speak to your father in that tone," my mother says. "Now apologize."

I look up at him my hands clenched at my side. "I'm sorry," I sob. But I am more furious than apologetic and I run from the room and out of the house.

It's decided. I'm going to teachers' college. Still three months shy of my twenty-first birthday, I can't enlist until I'm of legal age. To make my mother happy and to keep peace at home, I've agreed to go to Florence.

Boone and I are walking home from church, but stop at the Pender High School athletic field to talk about this latest news. He has played varsity football and run track on this field. At the 50-yard line we climb the wood bleachers all the way to the top and Boone sits a bench below me.

"I thought you were dead set on joining the WAACS."

"Mama said I owed it to the family to give college a try."

The full story is my mother has spent the last week talking separately to me and daddy to move us toward some middle ground.

"Well, I'm glad. You're not the kind of girl to be a WAAC. You remember Bertha Shepherd? She sent her brother a picture wearing her army uniform and smoking a cigar," Boone's head shakes in pure disgust. "Lil, do you hear what I'm saying?"

He gazes up at me with such earnestness. He has a newly grown mustache and looks older than his twenty-two years.

"I hear you but not all girl soldiers are, you know, funny like that. Some of them have boyfriends. I know I do," I say touching his face.

"Maybe they're not all like that but…"

13

"Please Boone, listen. All I know is that when I daydream I see myself walking in a city crowded with people who are all in hurry like they have some place to be. I have lots of friends-girls and guys-and we wear fine clothes and listen to jazz in fancy clubs where we laugh and talk and smoke cigarettes. In my dreams, my life is bigger."

Boone stares out at the football field. I don't usually share my imaginings with him. He and I both know they will eventually take me away but I can't hold back these longings, they pull on me throughout the day and I rarely escape them when I sleep. So I will go to my aunt's house and attend college but I haven't changed my mind. Once I come of age, I will join the WAACS. Not daddy, mama or Boone will talk me out of it.

"You know I love you, Boone."

"I know, Lil," he leans forward resting his head on my knee and I put my fingers into the deep nap of his hair.

"We better get going. Daddy will be looking for me and he knows you're walking me home."

"He's probably happy you're with me, at least it means you're not like one of them soldier girls," he teases.

Holding hands, we walk up the paved road that leads out of town and toward our farms. The elderly Harris twins, Miss Hattie and Miss Harriet, sit on their porch dressed in matching lavender and white dresses. They move back and forth in their rockers and the thin floor boards squeak with their movements blending with the screech of the cicadas. They wave when they see us and Miss Hattie, wearing her signature handkerchief pinned to the bodice of her dress, whispers something to her aging sister. They both giggle. When we reach the church and the cemetery the road's paving becomes hard-packed dirt. Boone's great grandmother and my daddy's parents and brother are buried here. We have deep attachments to Pender and to each other and I sense these may be our final days together in this familiar place.

The sticky air gathers dampness at my hairline and I dab at it with my hanky but Boone doesn't seem bothered by the humidity at all, his hand is cool and dry. I feel a strong comfort being with him as I always do but today I notice a bit more pressure in his grip.

Chapter 2

(LeRoy)

Nothing stirs on this stifling, late summer afternoon until a yellow jacket skirts past my ear breaking the stillness with its thin buzz. I swat at the insect and sweat forms on my forehead so I step from the porch into the yard hoping to catch a stray breeze. In the distance I see the silhouette of my father. He refers to his business as a hauling company but he is really a junk man and the heat has put an end to his work for the day. I hear him mumble as I walk toward him and he looks over his shoulder at the sound of my footsteps.

"Were you talking to yourself?"

He gives me a rare smile. "No, boy, I was praying. The pastor says to pray out loud...like Jesus did."

I'm surprised to hear my father speak of Jesus and wonder what troubles him enough to pray. I want to ask but it's too personal a question between strangers. When we talk it is awkward, discordant. I think we have both tried from time to time to be in tune but we have little in common except my mother loves us both.

My mother's religious devotion more than makes up for his lack. She believes being a member of Absalom Baptist Church is both an obligation and gift and her greatest pleasure comes from singing in the women's choir on the second Sunday of each month. Mother is twenty years younger than my father and in their wedding photo she was beautiful and strong, a tall, striking woman with flashing auburn eyes and full, brown curly hair. But she has been ill for many years and now looks older than him. A long time ago I asked my father why she was always sick. "When a woman loses a child sometimes her body just gives up hope," he'd said.

"How's your mother?"

"She's seems okay. She and ma'dear are crocheting a shawl for Mrs. Banneker. Her birthday is next Sunday," I add quickly hoping for a conversation. He nods.

I am a musician and as far as my father is concerned, a misfit. While the other boys spend their time skipping school, playing ball, and devising ways to either join or avoid the war, I practice my music. My father would sign up for the army today but he's too old to be in the war. He and I stand together in silence for a few more minutes but the sun gets the best of me and I return to the house to play my horn.

Music fills a deep space in my soul. It is the thing that gives me purpose but is a constant source of trouble between my mother and father. I don't know where she gets the money, but mother is faithful to purchase the money order for the $2.50 monthly rental for my trumpet and clarinet and mail it to a company in Atlanta. She gives me money for reeds and rosin and it is she who takes my side when band practice interferes with my home chores. "Sam," she says to my father, "that boy's got a gift and you're not gonna stand in the way of it." My father doesn't like it when she challenges him but on most other subjects she is so forgiving, never asking questions or complaining about his ways, so he gives in. Still when I practice music at home, a deep crevice creeps to his forehead and he retreats to the bedroom or outdoors. He has no use for music.

"Good LeRoy, very good," my music teacher says during band practice.

There is a school recital next week and I will play a trumpet solo on Gershwin's *An American in Paris*.

"Violins, you are coming in too late. Attack on your first down stroke and in the rest of the section, the music should be carefree."

Mr. Giles is a classically-trained pianist and serious about his job as the high school Music Director. Most of my fellow band members have taken this course because they think folk dancing is for losers, art appreciation is a waste of time, and band will be easy, but I'm in this class because I want to be a professional musician. Mr. Giles believes I can reach that goal and tutors me an hour each day after school.

"LeRoy, I fear the violin section will let us down during the recital."

"Yes sir," I am always surprised when he treats me like a colleague rather than a student. "But, I think Jenny is getting better so maybe you can try her as first violin instead of Arthur."

"That's a good idea, LeRoy," he says making a note in his book. "So, here's what I thought we would work on today, it's a trumpet arrangement for *Embraceable You*. Do you want to try it?"

I am eager to please Mr. Giles. I learn something new about music and life with every song he introduces to me. I pick up the sheet music and examine the notes and timing, then read the lyrics.

"You want to give it a go?" he asks.

In my seventeen years on earth I have not experienced the kind of love this song describes but it needs little help from me. When I'm done Mr. Giles has tears in his eyes.

"You are an expressive musician with a natural ability to capture the intent of a piece. I expect great things from you, LeRoy."

Mr. Giles likes me, and encourages me all the time. Just once, I'd like to feel that kind of support from my own father. A couple of years ago, out of the blue, father surprised me by taking me to the pool hall. My mother didn't think I was old enough but he told me to get my cap and as he was steering me out the door said: "He's got to grow up sometime, Artice."

Red's Pool Hall stinks of smoke, sweat and stale beer but it is the only place in Americus where a black man can let down his guard and relax in the company of other men. It is one large room with a high ceiling, a grimy storefront window and a cement floor painted black. A thin plywood bar held up with 2x4's takes up the long wall of the room, and assorted chairs and barrel tables are shoved against the opposite wall. In the rear is a green-felt pool table with a bare light bulb hanging above it from a rope.

The only good thing about Red's is a wondrous jukebox. It blares out all the popular music colored folks like to hear—the Duke, and Count Basie, the Song Spinners, Lionel Hampton and the Freddie Slack Orchestra. Soft amber glows from an oval window at its head revealing gold discs stacked like a king's treasure. Mahogany embraces its belly and the legs are covered with speckled, plastic columns in cream and gray. Except for Mr. Johnson's 1941 Studebaker coupe, and the stained glass at church, that juke is the most beautiful thing I've ever seen.

I intended to stay in front of the jukebox the entire night but my father came over and pointed his finger in my face. "Boy, you ain't ever gonna amount to anything if you don't get your head out of the clouds." He handed me a dime for a drink, and directed me to join the other boys who were gathered around the picture window.

I ordered an iced co'cola and Mr. Red—his name came from his freckles and rust-colored hair—used a metal opener hanging from a string on his belt to pry off the bottle cap. He asked if I wanted to drink from the bottle or wanted a glass and I chose the glass. He pulled an ice pick from his back pocket and chipped three small pieces from the block on the side of the bar then slowly poured the dark liquid over the ice. It foamed like beer so I pretended it *was* beer and leaned casually against the bar the way they do in cowboy movies.

I watched as my father circled the pool table then slapped two dimes onto its rim. One dime was for the use of the table, the other a challenge to his friends to match his bet.

"Who's ready for a beating?" he called out.

His buddies snorted and hooted their disagreement.

"Shucks, Dowdell, I don't know why you want to give your money away, but if you giving, I'm taking," one of his friend's shouted and the rear of the room filled with their laughter.

Eventually, I ambled over to the assortment of boys who were keeping an eye on Main Street. They talked about the war, baseball, cars and jostled each other to get a look at the girls who passed on their way to or from Annie B's beauty shop. I drank my co'cola and observed with fascination as they played the game of calling to the girls. They seemed to have as much fun when a girl stuck her nose in the air and hurried by, as when one slowed her walk to show off the movement of her hips.

"Look at that one, Butch" one of the guys said to the big fellow in the plaid shirt and blue jeans. "She was looking at you, man. Why don't you catch up with her and find out where she lives?"

"Aw, man I know that girl." Butch spoke lazily and took a swig from his bottle of root beer before he continued. He had an easy way about him and his muscles bulged under rolled flannel sleeves. "I can talk to her anytime I want, she's in my baby sister's class and is always trying to get me to look at her. But I ain't studying her."

I made efforts to participate in the fun. A couple of times I walked over to look at the spinning record on the juke box but each time I noticed my father watching me so I rejoined the boys. On the ride home, he and I were both caught up in our own thoughts. He was drunk and seemed to steer his truck over every hole on the dark road and when the truck dipped into a ditch I hit my head on the dashboard. By the time we got home both my head and stomach ached. I didn't mind that my father never took me to Red's again.

Mother is sick again and this time in the hospital, so ma'dear has moved in to take care of us. As usual my father doesn't want to talk about my mother's illness. Instead, he goes to Red's every night. Last night he came in late, and I heard him bumping into furniture and cursing so I got up to see if I could help. The front door was wide open and muddy footprints tracked from the door to the kitchen. Ma'dear was already turning on lights and taking in the whole scene. She gave my father a piece of her mind.

"Samuel, you ought to be ashamed of yourself. Artice is sick and you're out all hours of the night instead of being home with your son. You should hear what people are saying about you. I don't mind helping out," she paused to look at the mud. But I'll tell you one thing. I sure ain't cleaning up after a no-account drunk."

"You need to mind your own damn business, Katie Mae," my father yelled. So I tried to defend my grandmother.

"Daddy, you shouldn't talk to ma'dear that way."

That's when he lunged at me and grabbed me by the throat.

"Boy, don't you be challenging me."

His breath smelled of liquor and bile, and his watery eyes were locked on mine. I still remember my heart pounding in my ears as his hand tightened around my neck. Something told me not to resist and he finally loosened his grip.

He held out the palms of his hands, and turned to ma'dear whose face was gray with fear. She had been screaming and thrashing at my father all the time he held me in his grip, and now she took two steps back, clutching her robe tightly around her. My father fled through the open door.

My mother's bouts with gout have left her hair brittle and white, and her eyes like the inside of a seashell. She has returned home but my father still goes to town two nights a week and on those evenings I help with the dinner dishes and keep her company as she relaxes with her knitting. We sit side by side on the davenport and I tell her about my day at school. She wants to know all about my music classes and what Mr. Giles is teaching. Sometimes I'll play the songs on my clarinet. One is a favorite of hers and she sings along:

I'm always chasing rainbows, watching clouds drifting by. My schemes are just like all my dreams, ending in the sky. Some fellas look and find the sunshine; I always look and find the rain. Some fellas make a winning sometime, I never even make a gain; believe me. I'm always chasing rainbows, waiting to find a little blue bird, in vain.

The illness has left her with a lot of vibrato in her rich, alto and her voice breaks at the end of the song, but she seems to enjoy our opportunity to make music together. She smiles and makes jokes and, at least for those hours, seems like her old self.

I saw them together. My father and the woman who gives shampoos at Annie B's beauty salon. I was coming home from a

24

tutoring session with Mr. Giles and they turned down a side street arms entwined. She wore bright yellow shoes and a short black skirt and her hair was done up in a fancy way. My father was strutting like he does at the pool hall and after he leaned toward her ear, they both laughed loudly. He didn't see me, but I sure saw the two of them.

"Who was that woman you were with Tuesday evening? Walking up Morgan Street?" I ask.

I'm helping my father unload two old car engines he picked up out in the country. He doesn't respond to my question and points for me to grab one end of the second engine so we can carry it into the shed.

"Mama really misses you when you're away at night."

He wipes grease from his hands with a rag and shrugs his shoulders.

"There are some things about your mother and me you're too young to understand, LeRoy."

He is done talking and it is the most he has said to me in weeks. He can talk and smile with his pals at Red's, and with his woman friend, but I can barely get a 'good morning' from him.

"I've decided to join the army."

He nods. "I respect your decision. The war has given lots of boys the chance to leave their old lives and start new ones. A friend of mine is in the army. He says it's not an easy job, but it's a good way to find out what you're really made of."

I've also confided my plans to Mr. Giles, but I have other reasons for joining the army. One is to get away from my father, the other is to play more music. I've read Glenn Miller is forming a company of army musicians in New Jersey, and maybe I can be in his band.

"I don't fit in here, Mr. Giles…not even at home. My father doesn't like me. But, I hate to leave my mother."

My teacher looks at me with sympathy.

"As an artist it's important to be in an environment where your talents are supported. I'm grateful to have the appreciation of the church choir, and deserving students like you, LeRoy. But this is a town of small minds, and it's not a place to nurture big talent like you have."

I give some thought to what he says. He and mother know how important music is to me, but I don't think anyone else understands or even cares.

"Do you think I could get an assignment with one of the army bands, Mr. Giles?

"I've read about those bands. I don't know if they have military units of Negro musicians, but the world seems to be changing pretty fast so you never know. You just never know."

Chapter 3

(Georgette)

It is a beautiful, late August morning and I am a kite broken from its string. The Greyhound bus ride to Florence will take nearly four hours and most of the other passengers are asleep because it has been daylight only an hour but I'm too excited to rest. I am wearing my church shoes and Sunday dress and a small blue hat mama bought me just for this trip. This is an adventure and I'm eager to see the towns, houses and people that sweep by my window view. But a hand-painted recruiting sign on the roof of a barn shifts my mood. *Be a Girl with a Star-Spangled Heart* it reads, and I'm reminded that instead of heading off to see the world, I am bound for misery at the house of my Auntie Shirl.

There are not many vehicles on the highways because of the rationing of gas and rubber tires but even during war people have to travel and when the occasional automobile or truck passes, I lift myself up from the seat straining to see the passengers. An hour into the trip the bus overtakes an old pickup with four unkempt white children sitting in the truck bed. They see my head above the bus window and stick their tongues out at me. I lower myself back to the seat.

Daddy is uneasy around white people but I am just curious. I remember vividly, the incident two years ago where he acted

so strangely. He didn't work the farm for days. He and mama
whispered to each other when any of us girls were in earshot,
and he paced around the house and yard reminding me of our
cat, Ginger. On one of those afternoons, Mr. Johnson, Mr. Cato,
and Mr. Brownell came over and talked with my father for the
longest time. They squatted at the gravel turnoff in front of our
house and I eavesdropped from the open window, peeking
between the curtains.

"What if they come in the middle of the night, George?"
Mr. Cato ask daddy.

"Well, we just gonna have to be ready for them. We need to
stick together. It was probably one of those sailors from
Wilmington who raped that woman, not somebody from around
here."

I couldn't hear more of the conversation, but I kept my vigil.
Mr. Brownell scratched something in the dirt with a stick, and
finally the men rose to their feet and moved off in the direction
of their own farms. I drew away from the window when daddy
entered the front door, his face ashen and his eyes cold black.
He looked at me without really seeing me and went into the
kitchen to whisper something to mama. During supper that night
when we heard a truck speeding up the road, daddy jumped from
the table, almost knocking over his chair, and ran to the front of
the house. I followed-my mother's voice sounding my name-
just in time to see him turn off the table lamp, crouch to the floor

28

and push open the curtain at the window I'd spied from earlier that day. When daddy stood upright he left the lamp dark.

"Get back to the table and eat your supper, Sis," he'd said sternly, but I could tell he was more scared than angry.

I heard him tell Mr. Brownell the next morning, that he had stayed up all that night with his shotgun. Mr. Brownell said he had his gun at the ready, too.

"What else can we do with them crazy white folks all worked up?"

This morning, the view I have of the sixteen rows of white people seated in the front of the bus isn't frightening at all. Colored men, women, and children are in the last eight rows of the Greyhound and I have a seat to myself in the first row of our section. I take note of a young girl three rows up, she is traveling with two little boys and doesn't seem much older than me. The largest boy appears to be about three years old, and sits at the window seat on top of a brown suitcase with a red ribbon tied at the handle. I watch him climb off the luggage when the girl, who must be his mother, gets a diaper for the younger boy sitting on her lap.

A couple of soldiers are two rows directly in front of me. I noticed them when they put their duffel bags in the storage under the bus, and I watch them now with interest as they laugh and smoke cigarettes. They're both young and one of them looks a bit like Tyrone Power. I can't hear their conversation but imagine they are talking about their adventures and the different places they've seen. Suddenly, one turns in his seat and looks right at me. He says something to the other soldier who also shifts in his seat to stare. They share a throaty laugh then go back to their conversation. In that instant, I understand the fear my father felt two years ago.

It is nearing noon when the bus pulls to the curb in Florence. Right away I spot my Auntie Shirl wearing one of her large floppy hats. She is a short woman and, like all the women in my family, has wide hips made more pronounced today by the green and red floral dress she wears. I'm surprised so many passengers are leaving the bus at Florence—including the two soldiers and the girl with her sons. We all begin gathering our belongings. The girl manages to secure her suitcase under the arm that guides the restless toddler up the aisle, the other arm is full of the sleeping baby. The two soldiers see her efforts but just put on their caps, grab their black valises from the wire shelf above them, and depart the bus. I have my own small suitcase, filled with neatly folded blouses and skirts, undergarments and socks. I've also packed one pair of everyday lace-up shoes and a couple of gifts for Auntie Shirl. I offer the girl my help.

"I can take the suitcase for you miss. I have a free hand."

The girl is too overburdened to refuse my assistance.

"Thank you," she sighs. "Could you just help me get Zeke down the stairs of the bus, girlie?" She sees my changed expression at her use of the word 'girlie'.

"I sure do appreciate it."

Zeke is a handful. He wriggles and yanks on my arm trying to free himself from my grip. He even tries to bite my hand as we move down the aisle. "Zeke if you don't behave yourself, I'll be telling your daddy," his mother warns and he seems to understand the seriousness of his situation because he settles right down. When we get to the sidewalk I loosen my hold on the boy's hand, and we wait as his mother balances her way down the three steps of the bus. Auntie Shirl sees me, starts waving, and takes a few steps toward me then her arm slowly drops when she notices the boy. She looks confused but says nothing. She stops in her tracks and gawks.

"Okay, Zeke we're going to gramps' house now," the girl says.

She nods her thanks to me takes her son's hand and walks into the bus depot. My aunt watches as if it is a Hollywood movie.

"Hello, Auntie Shirl."

"Well...Well," she stammers. "Did you have a good trip?"

"Yes Auntie."

31

"I see that you met some people on the bus." Her statement is part question, part accusation.

"Yes Auntie."

I don't want to give her any cause for criticism so I say no more.

"Well, Georgette, I see you haven't changed very much, you're more grown up but you still have that sour attitude. How are your mother and your sisters?"

Auntie Shirl rarely inquires about daddy's wellbeing. She thinks he *also* has a sour attitude.

"Everyone is fine, Auntie. Mama sends her love and two jars of her strawberry preserves."

"And my girl, Helen, how is she doing?" Auntie purrs.

We all know Helen is my aunt's pet, but it still hurts that she loves my middle sister so much more than me, Barbara, or even our little sister, Ruthie. "Georgette surely takes after her daddy, but Helen looks more and more like mama, every day," Auntie Shirl usually says at our family gatherings. Which means that fifteen-year-old Helen looks like Auntie Shirl whose light complexion, thin nose, and small lips are coveted by many in our race. Mama rarely takes part in these comparisons, but when she does it is simply to say: "I believe you're right, Shirl, all my girls have very nice facial features."

"Helen is doing well," I finally reply to my aunt's question. "So are Barbara and Ruthie...and daddy," I add stubbornly.

32

Auntie Shirl raises one eyebrow, her face frozen in displeasure. "Well, let's get your bag and get on home."

My aunt lives alone in a spacious, three-story house five miles outside of Florence. Uncle Ray, a member of the Brotherhood of Sleeping Car Porters, died in 1940 in a work accident, and his life insurance has left her quite well off by the standards of the day. The house has abundant windows and a big front porch. Uncle Ray built a room onto the back of the house with a bathtub and indoor toilet—not every house in a community this small has such luxuries. A narrow stairwell off the dining room leads to the third-floor attic where I am to sleep—a retreat from Auntie Shirl, and hers from me.

One whole side of the attic is furnished as a spare bedroom. There is a white, three-drawer dresser, a large oak desk, an old but comfortable stuffed chair, and an iron-framed bed covered with a blue and white gingham quilt. A single bulb hanging from a cord on the slanted ceiling provides a dim light and casts shadows on the rafters at night but during the day there is abundant light from two, arched windows. Three links of heavy chain, anchored to one of the ceiling beams, holds a pole from which dark blue drapes hang and I can draw them together to separate my bed from the sitting area. A small nook cut into a side wall serves as a door-less closet with a single shelf, several hooks, and a piece of wire nailed at both ends to hold a few

33

wood hangers. The room's finishing touch was a white loop rug between the dresser and the bed.

At home, I shared a bedroom with Barbara so I love this space that I can call my own. I will pay for my room and board by keeping my space clean, helping Auntie Shirl with laundry and doing some outdoor chores. It's more than a fair trade after my routine of hard farm work. For the first time in my life I feel like an independent woman.

"Hi mama, yes, everything is fine. I miss you too."

It has been ten days since I left Pender and I've called home three times. Many houses in the south still don't have telephones but Auntie's does—it just doesn't come with privacy. So today I'm using the call box at Grayson's Five-and-Dime.

"Sis, you got everything you need?" Mama uses her louder than normal, long-distance voice.

"Yes ma'am, my room is nice and I have a desk and everything," I brag.

I don't mention that Auntie Shirl is already getting on my nerves. A man steps up to the call box and looks in, his eyes asking how long I'll be. I hold up my index finger signaling that I need a bit more time. I turn my back to him.

"Yes, I start school on Wednesday and tomorrow I have to register for my classes. Uh huh, the street car drops me off very nearby. No, I'm calling from the drugstore in town, I needed a few things. What? Oh, I will mama, don't worry. I'll be sure to call you next week, please kiss Barbara, Helen and Ruthie for me. What? Oh, yes tell daddy, I love him, too."

I want to ask my mother about Boone but I don't. He said he would write. I haven't received a letter yet and I've already written to him twice.

When I step off the street car near the Linwood Normal School for Colored Girls, a wave of fear mixed with anticipation passes through my body. Summer has given way to milder weather and a few of the maple trees are beginning to hint at their fall colors, but the sky is a clear blue and the short walk from the bus to the college calms me. I spot Linwood as soon as I turn off the main street, it is grand like something out of one of my magazines. A green plaque with gold leaf on the wrought-iron gate proclaims 1882 the date of Linwood's founding by the Quakers and the local AME church. Through the gate I see a broad white building with tall columns and stained glass windows. Black trees drooping with moss hug the path to the center of the campus. Arrow signs with the word 'registration' point to the main building and as I step deeper into the grounds I see smaller buildings dotted along grassy meadows on both sides.

There are lots of girls...some in pairs or small groups but many alone, like me. I see all kinds of hair-dos from bobs to long hair, good hair to nappy. Most of the girls wear medium-length skirts or dresses, sturdy shoes with white socks and some have small hats. I've worn my Sunday clothes and fit right in. I pause when a late-model, dark-blue, Ford moves slowly up the horseshoe driveway and stops at the entrance of the main building. A very pretty girl wearing stylish clothes and carrying a book bag gets out of the automobile. This is not Howard University or Spelman College but the ladies who come to Linwood are from families who want their daughters to have choices in life. I guess I should feel lucky to be here.

My footsteps echo when I enter the Frederick Douglass Hall where registration is underway. I let out a small gasp at the sight of a massive chandelier. It has a tiny lamp shade for each bulb, I count twenty lights. Directly below the chandelier is the largest carpet I've ever seen, a blood-red border surrounds a pattern of blue, white and yellow squares in the center. As I step onto the rug I realize the design is a series of panels depicting an ancient civilization. They show beautiful gold buildings, long boats with sails, and dark skin people in elaborate robes, some wearing crowns others riding camels. The walls of the great hall are covered in cherry wood from floor to ceiling. The floors are green and white marble, green velvet drapes are tied back at the windows of lead and stained glass, each pane illustrating a major scene from the Bible.

My nerves are back. I feel like a naïve country girl in this room and I timidly join the registration line clutching my handbag and the check it holds. Daddy was so proud to give me this check and three others, along with the ledger book that shows the balance in my first bank account. These funds are to be spent only for school. I'll find work to pay for any extras I need or want.

The man at the registration counter is older than me but younger than my parents. He wears black-rimmed eyeglasses, a white shirt, blue bow-tie and a red and black sweater vest and he smiles as he hands me a piece of paper and a pencil.

"Fill out this form over there, young lady," he points a finger across the room to three rows of folding chairs facing four, large blackboards. Each blackboard has a list of courses, class times and teacher names neatly printed in yellow chalk. "You're a freshman so you should pick one class from each board," he directs. "When you've completed your form, please bring it back to me."

"Where do I pay my money?" I ask shyly and he smiles again.

"Come back to this line to pay your tuition after I review your registration form," he dismisses me to wait on the girl behind me.

The registration process takes three hours and there is a lot of waiting. Some of the girls have brought light lunches of sandwiches and fruit and some have books to read. I didn't think to bring anything to pass the time so I take a closer look at the room. There are portraits of the co-founders of Linwood. Three of the portraits are of the two men and one woman who were Quakers but the rest are prominent Negro men and women. I recognize a few names: Mary McLeod Bethune, Asa Philip Randolph and Harriet Tubman. Others I've never heard of before like Garret Morgan and Benjamin Banneker.

The registration clerk looks over my form. "You have American Lit, American History 1, World Geography 1 and the first section of Latin. Good," he says and stamps my form.

I fill in the check for my tuition payment. I've received A's throughout elementary, middle and high school for my petite cursive. The clerk looks at the check carefully.

"You're from Pender County, I see. I know it."

He gives me a look of memory and kindness. I want to ask him how and when he managed to escape Pender but I can't get up the nerve.

"Everything looks in good order, Miss Newton," he says stamping my receipt. "You are now officially a student at Linwood College. Good luck."

Auntie Shirl is friends with one of the administrators at Linwood who has arranged a job for me in the school cafeteria. My shift starts at 11 a.m. on Mondays, Wednesdays and Thursdays when I help set up the serving area for lunch, later I spoon out food from hot chafing dishes onto the plates of waiting diners. I am off duty no later than 2 p.m. and for three hours of work, I receive ninety cents and a free lunch. My pay for the week is almost three dollars from which I save a dollar, tithe thirty cents and use the rest for toiletries, stamps, the drug store pay phone and a weekly magazine.

I've already made a few friends like Henrietta who I met at the five-and-dime, and Selena and Catherine who are in my literature class. American Lit is my favorite course because our professor, Dr. Ronald Adams, makes the class interesting by mixing classic works with the poetry and fiction of newer writers. Dr. Adams is not real old like some of the other professors and he's visited Paris, Rome and lived in Washington, DC.

"How many of you have heard of the Harlem Renaissance?"

A half-dozen girls raise their hands.

"Only a few of you, I see. Well the term refers to a cultural movement by a group of artists, musicians and writers whose creative themes focus on the Negro experience in America and abroad. During this course we'll be reading and discussing a

39

number of their contemporary offerings as well as the work of more established American authors."

Professor Adams loves books and speaks of them as if they were people he knows, even friends. The teachers at Pender High School made us read *Little Women* and *Huckleberry Finn* but those stories never came to life for me the way they have in Adams' class and he's also introduced us to Negro writers like Zora Neale Hurston and poet, Countee Cullen.

"Dr. Adams is a dreamboat, isn't he?" Selena has a serious crush on the professor. She cups her face in her hands and looks moon-eyed.

It's Thursday, late afternoon, and Selena, Catherine and I are doing homework. Henrietta is not in our American Lit class but has joined us for the gossip, and to hear about the books we've read. Because I work in the cafeteria, and Chef likes me, he allows us to gather at one of the tables as long as we like, and he brings over a pot of tea and four delicious slices of rhubarb pie.

"What do you think of Zora Neale, Georgette?" Catherine asks.

"I wish I was her. Traveling around and meeting new people all over the world."

My new friends are already familiar with my habit of daydreaming about being someplace other than where I am.

"I don't know if I understand her writing but I sure do like her style," Selena says finishing off her pie. "She wears amazing hats."

"Who is she?" Henrietta asks.

Adams has spent two classes lecturing about Hurston's life and work, and I tell Henrietta everything I know and have heard of Zora Neale. Of all the authors we've discussed in class, she is the one who has most captured my imagination. I'm grateful for the discussions at Linwood about books and the faraway places and situations they describe. I would never have these conversations at home, still I'd rather be *having* these experiences than talking about them.

Boone has finally written. His letter is filled with news about our friends and acquaintances and I'm reading it again curled up in my stuffed chair in the attic. His father got an infection after being cut in an accident with his tractor so Boone has taken over all the work of the farm—and he likes being in charge. Colored recruiters spoke to the church congregation two weeks ago and his best friend, Curtis, joined the army on the spot. Boone's mother and father celebrated their 25th wedding anniversary with a big party and almost every colored family in town came, including my parents. The last page of Boone's letter is for the personal stuff. He says he misses me and has meant to write sooner but is tired after working all day, every day. 'Besides,' he writes, 'I thought you would probably be

41

busy with your new college friends.' I know he really means college boys.

Before I left, Boone and I agreed we would remain boyfriend and girlfriend unless one of us decided to break it off. Boone's letter makes it sound as if he is too busy to see other girls but I know his nature. I also know Bobbie Briscoe's sister, LuAnn, has her sights set on him. As for me, I already know Linwood is not the place I will meet the dapper men in my daydreams, most single men my age have either enlisted in the military or been drafted.

I tuck Boone's letter into my sweater pocket, and pick up a *Look* magazine. There is no more daylight to stream into the attic, so I switch on the overhead bulb. As usual, the pictures and stories in *Look* remind me of a life I don't have...but not for much longer.

Chapter 4

(LeRoy)

This morning, I am to report for army duty. I sit on the side of my mother's bed, hold her hand, and watch her cry.

"Your father has always done the best he knew how," her voice is hoarse. "Please don't think too badly of him, LeRoy, he really is a man of God."

I nod. "Yes, ma'am, but he makes me feel like an unwelcome guest."

I don't want to leave my mother in such a lonely house. My father isn't around this morning but when I announced last week that I was leaving for the army he didn't ask any questions, and said: "Well, that's man's work at a time when it's needed."

I walk the five dusty miles to the bus station leaving behind the streets and houses of my boyhood. I have a carpetbag with a few possessions and a small cornmeal bag stuffed with food that ma'dear has prepared for me. The bag is heavier with each mile. I pass through the colored business section. Anna B's salon isn't yet open, and neither is Red's, but I see people in the shoe repair shop and after I cross the railroad track I see more people leaving the building where Western Union and the bank do business. Next to it is the bus depot. I already have my ticket so I sit on the bench in front. I've only been sitting a few minutes when I see my father walking towards me from across the street.

He has his hat pulled low on his head, and his hands are deep in the pockets of his brown corduroy jacket. He reaches the bench and sits, but doesn't look at me. I instinctively put some space between us.

"LeRoy," he says in greeting.

"Morning sir," I reply. I haven't called him father in a long time.

We sit in our usual silence. After a time he pulls out his worn, black billfold and I stare at his thick-knuckled fingers as he works them through the contents of the wallet. He finds what he is looking for and hands it to me. A small photograph of me and mother. In it, I am about four years old and perched on her lap. She looks beautiful in a long dark skirt and a blouse with a high collar. Her hair is up in a bun and a ribbon is tied around her neck. I wear a shirt with matching shorts and a small sailor's cap. I'm smiling. I have seen this photo before but I had no idea my father carries it around with him. "Keep that picture to remember your mama by," he says. He puts the wallet away and reaches into his shirt pocket for a stick of Black Jack chewing gum which he splits in half and hands to me. He removes a large, wrinkled handkerchief from the back pocket of his coveralls, dingy from sweat mixed with red clay. He blows his nose loudly then puts the handkerchief away and stares at his old work boots.

The bus turns onto Main Street and comes to a stop in front of the bench. A couple and a single lady exit. The couple start up the street to the white section of town while the colored lady turns the opposite way. The driver eyes me and my bag so I stand and show him my ticket.

"Joining the army, I see." He looks at the front and back of the travel voucher. "We'll be leaving in a few minutes. If you want you can put your bag in the bottom of the bus."

My father and I stand awkwardly together not knowing what to do next. We take turns glancing at each other and then away.

"Well, sir. I'll be seeing you." I offer my father a handshake and he accepts.

"I'll be seeing you too, son. I'll take care of your mother, you can be sure of that."

I watch as he ambles across the street, climbs into his truck and drives off in the direction of home. Later, when I think of my final conversation with my father, I will look at that old, sepia photo and remember the day he called me son.

The bus takes me to Tallahassee where I am to board a recruit transport—another bus. There are twenty of us headed to basic training in Arizona, and we are a lively bunch. Almost all have been drafted but I lied about my age—just a month shy of eighteen—when I signed up. Most of the guys are from South

Carolina and Florida, but there is one other recruit from Georgia. He calls himself Pit, he is a big guy with a voice like a bass drum, and a personality to match. We hit it off right away.

After the get-to-know-you's, we pull out the good food our mamas, and grandmas, and aunts, have prepared for the first part of our long journey—fried chicken and biscuits, ham hocks, peach cobbler, and baked sweet potatoes stuffed with butter. Pit hasn't brought any food so I share my grandmother's home cooking with him. An hour later, we are full and there is a sense of fun as if we are all heading out on a fishing trip. We tell jokes and laugh, sing a few songs and wave at those we see through the bus windows. When night falls, the driver announces we are riding through Alabama. The bus is quiet and dark, the only light comes from a bit of moon and swarms of lightning bugs in the thick woods on either side of the two-lane road. It is the first time I have been so long from Americus. A couple of times my father and I have driven to my uncle's place in Sumter to help him and my cousins pick peaches, but that was only for a couple of days and Americus was not so far away.

A stray enters our back yard and Trout, protecting his territory, confronts the mangy, black dog. The hair on the back of my 12-year-old neck prickles, and a high-pitched bell sounds in my ears. The two dogs snarl at each other with wild eyes and teeth bared. In a matter of seconds they lunge, each trying to pierce long teeth into the other's jugular. My father darts from

46

the shed into the yard. The black dog strikes first, catching Trout's floppy, yellow ear and upper jaw. It is a bad bite and blood surges from the place where Trout's ear hangs by a string of flesh. The growls and yelps continue as father hits the stray with a branch he's yanked from our willow tree. He yells for me to bring a bucket of water from the trough. "Throw it, LeRoy. Throw it, boy," he hollers. The water hits right into the middle of them two dogs and they stop, momentarily stunned. The black dog jumps at my head and I raise my arm to protect my face. Father charges the stray, swinging the tree branch and sending him running but not before the dog gets hold of the knuckle on my little finger. I watch scarlet spread across my fingers and hear my father moan low in his throat. Trout lies on the ground. His breathing is short, and his tongue hangs out the way it does on sticky summer days. My father lifts Trout's head onto his lap, it is the only time I have seen him cry and he takes no notice that I cradle my bleeding hand as he lifts Trout from the dirt and carries him into the barn. I follow, kneeling over the whimpering dog and he looks up at me, his eyes asking forgiveness for not protecting us, for letting that black stray get the best of him. My father yanks me up by the back of my shirt, pushes me behind him with one, strong arm and shoots our old yella' dog right in the place where his ear had been.

I awake with a cry from this nightmare I have had many times before. I look around the bus to see if anyone has heard me but everyone seems to be sleeping. It is almost dawn. My lips are chap, my throat is dry and I have to pee. In a while I know we'll pick up food and then a few minutes later the driver will pull the bus over to the loose gravel on the side of the road for our break. This schedule is what our army escort, Corporal Sneed calls 'routine'. Like clockwork, at six a.m., noon, and six p.m. we stop for our meal then drive on for a pee break. We don't leave the bus to eat at the road diners and rest stops because—soldiers or not—they won't serve coloreds. So the white bus driver grabs his cap and a pouch with the meal vouchers and goes into these establishments alone to purchase food. Sneed stays with us on the bus, he is colored but makes no attempt to associate with us. He exchanges an occasional word with the driver but mostly he slumps in his seat with his cap pulled over his eyes.

Ten minutes later we stop for breakfast somewhere near Hattiesburg, Mississippi. The driver goes into the diner and we bide our time. One of the guys, Brewster, announces to Corporal Sneed that he really has to pee and is leaving the bus—I'm thinking of joining him.

"That's against the rules, recruit," Sneed says barely looking up.

"I know," Brewster says politely, "but I just gotta go now."

Before Sneed can stop him, Brewster pushes open the bus door and jumps to the ground. We watch as he trots to a thick

48

group of bushes at the side of the diner. He glances left and right then turns his back to the road. Out of nowhere, three white men appear with shotguns and surround him. Without a word, one of them hits Brewster in the back of the head with the butt of his gun. We all cry out in alarm and several guys bolt for the bus exit.

"Sit your asses down," Sneed screams and blocks the door

"You'll get us all killed."

"But one of them crackers just hit Brewster in the head," Pit challenges Sneed.

"I saw it Turner, but I'm in charge here and you'll do as I say."

Sneed quickly tucks in the shirt of his uniform, squares his hat and steps off the bus.

"What seems to be the problem, sirs?" his voice has an easy tone.

The three white men turn their heads to look at Sneed but keep their shotguns aimed at Brewster who is kneeling and holding a hand to his head.

"The problem is this nigger is trespassing," we hear one of the men say, ignoring Sneed's uniform but not his question.

"Well sir, he's just a new army recruit and he don't know yet, how to follow orders. We're taking this bunch to Arizona for basic training."

"Army niggers, you say," one of the men drawls looking Sneed up and down and then peers at our green bus.

As if someone gives a signal, we all draw back from the windows and hold our breath not knowing what to expect next. I can almost feel the man's bloodshot eyes on my black face. The driver leaves the diner carrying a packing crate filled with food and stops short when he sees the armed men talking to Sneed and Brewster on the ground. Sizing up the situation quickly, he hands the crate of food to Sneed and beckons for him to get back on the bus. We all watch the driver and the three men for a full five minutes as they talk in low voices. They are not young men, one has a graying beard, another chews and spits tobacco. They all wear overalls, and denim caps like those worn by train engineers. After some time, one by one, the men position their guns away from Brewster's head. They laugh with the driver, and point a few times in the direction our bus is traveling. The driver doesn't wear an army uniform but he is white and that seems to be the only authority he needs in this part of the Deep South. Finally, the men walk toward the rear of the diner and out of our view.

The driver helps Brewster to his feet, then he and Sneed guide him onto the bus and into the first seat. The driver whispers something to the corporal, and puts the bus back on the road. Sneed distributes the bags of food but no one eats. When we've gone up the road a mile or so the driver pulls the bus over, and we watch him retrieve a first-aid kit from under his seat and remove a bottle. Rubbing alcohol stings our noses, as he soaks a wad of cotton gauze and secures it on Brewster's wound with tape. Sneed stands in the aisle, clears his throat, and makes a little speech.

"There is a reason for our routine, recruits," he begins, "what happened to Brewster back there could happen to anyone of you if you don't follow orders and observe the routine."

Corporal Sneed continues with his explanation of regulations like he's memorized it from some book. The urge to pee returns, and I wish he would hurry up, but just then Brewster gives a loud groan. I think maybe I'll take the corporal's words to heart.

When we began this trip we were carefree, laughing, joking and sometimes singing and I'd accompany the songs by beating out rhythms on the back of the seat with my fingers, or playing on my trumpet mouthpiece. We encouraged anyone who wanted to sing a solo, and a couple of guys had voices as good as Billy Eckstine or Nat Cole. But for the last day-and-a-half, the sense of fun is gone and the guys have been pretty quiet. The Brewster incident has left all of us aware of our real situation— we might be starting a new part of our lives, but the old ways are still with us.

I push the thoughts of our close call out of my head by thinking about music. I want to play swing music in a big band like the one led by Tommy Dorsey. I have no idea how I will make this happen, but I've been well prepared by Mr. Giles. I'm lucky to have had him as a teacher.

In addition to teaching music at my school, Bonaparte Giles is the organist and choir director at our church. He took on those jobs when he returned to Americus from Chicago a few years ago to look after his ailing seventy-three year old mother. He is nothing like the other colored men in town. He still remembers the lessons of growing up in a small community, but his style is all big-city doings. He wears fancy suits to church—one for choir practice and a different one for Sunday service. His dress shoes are always polished to a bright sheen, and he has a collection of bow ties with patterns of stripes, polka dots and little swirls. He brings his mother to church service, pushing her wheel chair right up to one of the front pews, then takes his place at the organ with the flair of a concert pianist.

My mother speaks well of Mr. Giles because of his attentiveness to his own mother and because he is a patient choir director, but my father dislikes the man. I recall one conversation where he made that very clear. He had asked me a rare question about my trumpet playing and I told him Mr. Giles thought I was good enough to be a professional musician if I continued to work hard. My father stared at me for a couple of beats before saying, "Playing music ain't work, it's just what it says, 'play'. That Giles is soft. He ain't done a day of man's work in his life."

It's true, Mr. Giles has no interest in manual labor, and is not at all handy when it comes to the upkeep of the old two-story clapboard he shares with his mother. The kitchen sink is still fitted with a pump instead of faucets, the roof has holes in four or five places where even the lightest rain can drip onto the floor, and his porch has dry rot. But those things don't concern him because he has the only necessity that matters—a phonograph, and the wonderful collection of 78 rpm records he plays on it. He could sell the machine, and the records, to any one of the white families in town for money to patch his roof, or lay gravel on his dirt walkway, but I've heard him say many times that life would be unbearable without his Victrola.

I am his star music pupil at Junction Secondary School, and often visit with him and his mother on Sunday afternoons to listen to whatever new record he's purchased. Sounds from heaven pour through his parlor when he places the large needle of the Victrola into the grooves of the shiny black discs. I sit in one of his shabby arm chairs, lean back into the bumpy cushion and just let the music flow over me. "That one is by a Russian cat by the name of Tchaikovsky," he might explain excitedly. Mr. Giles loves the language of jazz and be-bop, even when he's describing other kinds of music, and uses words like "solid" and "cool" all the time. I prefer swing music but classical music is good too. "Listen to the French horns and cellos, LeRoy," Mr. Giles will say and I open my eyes to see him pacing the floor and jabbing the air with his pipe, as if directing the orchestra. "Isn't it lovely? Doesn't it make your heart soar?"

When I hear a trumpet playing staccato over the hard beat of the traps, my pulse quickens like it does when I watch the girls at school play volleyball in their gym shorts, or when I see Butch without his shirt. But symphony music gives me a different feeling. It's like I'm floating in clouds.

The bus hits a deep hole and shakes me back to the present. The other recruits are napping, reading, or just looking out the window. A few are playing a game of cards. Pit looks back at me from the front of the bus where he's been sitting with Brewster. All this quiet must be hard on someone like Pit. I give him a nod to let him know I'm awake and he comes back to join me.

"Hey LeRoy, ain't you ready to get off this bus?"

"It wasn't so bad at first, but now I want to get where we're going. Hey, how is Brewster doing?"

"He's got a big knot on his head, and he's eating aspirin by the handful but I think he's gonna live."

"I gotta tell you Pit that stuff back there, with those white men, scared the crap out of me. I guess I was thinking, you know, everybody would respect us because we're soldiers."

"If they just let me in the fight, LeRoy, I'll show them what colored soldiers can do. I can't wait to kill some Nazis and some of them Japs."

I'm pretty sure I don't want to kill anybody, and I know I didn't want anybody to kill me but I keep that to myself.

"Hey man, where'd you learn to play music?" Pit asks.

"I learned at school. I play trumpet, saxophone, clarinet, French horn, I can even play the oboe."

Pit seems impressed, but quickly changes the subject.

"I'm a ball player myself, you ever play ball?"

Pit and I are about the same age, but I realize he knows a lot more than me about living life. For the next two hours, I listen to his stories about triumph in baseball, football…and with women.

Our bus rolls into Texas two days later, and I see what the driver tells us are Indians but they sure aren't like the ones in the Gene Autry westerns. They don't have war paint, or feathers, or teepees. They live in short houses that are a brownish-red color and the windows don't have any glass. They have the same brown skin as my Aunt Hazel's kids, except they have good hair, all shiny, black, and straight. Usually the kids we see on the road—even white kids—wave at our bus when it streaks by their houses, schools and fishing spots, and we wave back happy to recall the freedom of childhood. But these brown kids don't

55

wave they just stare at us as if they can read some story of days gone by in our faces.

We stop for lunch and the driver returns with our meals of a big meat bone with brown beans and rice, and instead of real cornbread there is fried corn mush. One of the fellas says it is a corn cake. I throw mine out the window and before it can even get dirt on it, one of them Indian kids picks it up and bites it in half. He is barefoot and a rag is tied across his forehead to keep his hair behind his ears. His little brown pants hang big on him, so he has another rag around his waist to holding up his britches. He looks right in my eyes while he eats the corn cake and I stare back. An old woman comes out of one of the stone houses and says something to him. She speaks real fast-in words I've never heard before-and the kid jerks his eyes away from me and runs to the house, but he doesn't drop that bread.

At suppertime we pull into a military base and gratefully leave the bus we've been on for five-and-a-half days. After standing in line for an hour, we board the rear compartments of a crowded troop train. We are now with dozens of other colored soldiers, some recruits like us, others in full uniform. The driver leave us but Corporal Sneed accompanies us on the train, and there are porters—older, colored men—who bring us coffee and make sure we get our evening meal. Sneed seems to have buddies among the other escorts and I watch them talking near the door of the train. When he points out Brewster to the group they form a tight circle and cigarette smoke twirls above them. They steal glances at Brewster and shake their heads.

After dinner, I study sheet music for the song *It Had to be You*, a composition by Isham Jones. Without warning, a wave of fear comes over me and I tremble. I wonder if I've made a mistake in joining the army. I look around the compartment to see if anyone else looks nervous, but they all seem to be having a good time. I spot Pit in the middle of a group of men telling stories and making everyone laugh. My anxiousness must have shown because a porter comes to my rescue.

"Can I get you a cup of coffee, young man?"

"No. No thank you."

"Is this your first train trip?"

I don't answer because if I try to speak my emotions will betray me. So I nod.

"There are some empty seats in the next car. It's quieter back there, and you could clear your head or maybe catch a few winks. I've worked on a lot of these troop trains, and sometimes they can get so noisy a man can't even think his own thoughts."

"That would be good," I say thankful for the opportunity to be alone.

"What's your name, young man?"

"LeRoy Dowdell."

"Well, come on Mr. Dowdell, I'll take your bag and show you the way."

I didn't realize I'd been clutching my carpetbag to my chest until the porter reaches for it. He smiles and I follow him through the crowded car. My legs are unsteady and I grip the back of the seats as we walk in the opposite direction of the train's movement. A few guys glance our way but nobody takes much notice. The next car is full, but the one after is nearly empty and I settle into a seat.

For hours, I stare out the window at the shapeless landscape. *'It had to be you, it had to be you. I've wandered around, finally found the somebody who'* The song lyric tumbles around in my head. *'Could make me be true, could make me be blue.'* Finally, the sound of the track carries me to dreams of chirping insects, and the clicks of crochet needles.

The next morning we arrive at our destination—Fort Huachuca Army Base near Tucson, Arizona. As I step from the train I have to shield my eyes from the intensity of the sun. Corporal Sneed directs us to a fenced off area where we wait and watch hundreds of soldiers, white and colored, move on and off the train. In ten minutes the train's whistle blasts once, and then once again, before it continues west, bound for California.

A thin layer of dust makes my eyes sting and invades my clothes, skin and hair. The smell of diesel fuel, mixed with some rotting animal, assaults my nostrils. Home is alive with color—in the trees, insects and birds, but everything I see here at this desert fort—fences, rocks, the scraggly shrubs in the distance, even the spiders, appear used up and colorless like a field of corn harvested and plowed over. The hot air seeps up through the beige ground in waves, and only the Huachuca Mountains, a far-off shimmering boundary on three sides of the base, offer harmony to the strains of sand and heat.

We're told to line up in four rows, and Pit heads to the front row. His given name is Jerome Turner but 'Pit' has stuck to him because as a boy he loved peaches and always had pocketsful of pits, which he used in his sling shot to pick off birds. I watch him from the second row, joking with the guys who flank him and holding court. One of the colored sergeants—his shiny name tag read 'Moses'—also watches Pit and then approaches him.

"Where are you from recruit?" Sgt. Moses asks.

"Well, Sergeant," Pit drawls and turns sideways so he has the audience of the guys behind him. "I'm from a place with the prettiest women and the sweetest peaches you ever seen. It's called Bluffton, Georgia. Sound good to you, Sarge?"

Pit flashes a smile of straight teeth and he gives me a wink. A few of the guys echo his laugh. But Sergeant Moses isn't amused. He takes a step forward to stand toe-to-toe with Pit then says in a tone as dangerous as a switchblade: "Well, boy there are no peaches at Huachuca, and if it's your girlfriend or your mama you're missing you'll get to see her real soon because a corn-pone farm nigger like you probably won't last long in this man's army."

The sergeant's words end in a sneer set in stone on his face. Pit and the rest of us don't move, stunned by the hatred we feel from this man who could have been cousin to any one of us but who spit out the word 'nigger' in a way we have only heard from white lips. Pit's face is red, and a vein in his neck twitches but he doesn't react. Where most of us come from a man only speaks to another man like that if he doesn't care whether he lives or dies, and none of us has yet seen or heard enough to want to die in this unfamiliar desert.

"You got more to say, farm boy?" Sgt. Moses asks.

Pit's hands form two large fists. "No."

"I didn't think so."

Chapter 5

(Georgette)

My visit home found things mostly unchanged. Mama and daddy were happy to see me. My sisters have adjusted to handling my chores, and Barbara loves having her own room, but she didn't mind making space for me again for a few days.

As I feared, LuAnn Briscoe was trying hard to capture Boone's affections. He joined our family for Sunday dinner but left early because he had arranged to have dessert with the Briscoe's. "I told you, Lil, it would be rude to cancel now. I promised LuAnn I would be there," Boone had said, but he knew I was angry and the next day he took off early from the farm to spend time with me. We visited with his folks, and drove into Wilson for a movie. In the theatre, we sat in the last row, held hands, and stole kisses whenever the movie screen was dark.

I'm grateful mama reminded me to pack my winter coat for my return to Linwood. I have only a short walk to the bus stop, but it is very cold. The black trees on the path to the main gate have lost their moss and cast lean shadows on the pavement. The few people who remain on campus move quickly to their destinations.

Boone is still on my mind when I arrive at Auntie Shirl's house and I take a deep breath of cold air before I open the door. I am at Linwood six or more hours a day, but tensions with my aunt have not lessened. She is critical of what I wear, how I fix my hair, and my habit of reading magazines. "Real life is passing you by while you're daydreaming with those periodicals Georgette," she always complains. She'd be happy if I spent more time hobnobbing with her snooty church friends, but I don't like most of them. They aren't regular like the people in our church at home.

As usual, Auntie Shirl and I cannot eat supper without her nagging about something I am, or am not, doing. The truth is, she is intent on marrying me off to Randall Whitten, the son of one of her old cronies.

"Georgette, I don't understand why you don't want to go out again with Mrs. Whitten's son. He comes from a good family and he's going to make a name for himself someday."

"I think he's stuck up Auntie. I know other girls who have been out with him, and they all say the same thing, he thinks he's some kind of Casanova."

"You must be exaggerating. I saw him in town yesterday, and he especially asked about you. Why, he seems like such a quiet, studious boy."

Quiet, my foot. I never bothered to tell Auntie Shirl that I spent the entire two-and-a-half hours of my date with Randall, fighting off his advances. There are rumors that before he gets some girl in trouble, his mother is hoping to find a wife for him—that won't be me.

62

"Auntie Shirl, I already have a boyfriend. You remember Boone?"

"I remember him," she says turning up her nose. "His daddy has that farm up the road. I thought you were too good for the farm."

"I never said that. I just want to see what else the world has to offer."

"Well you're not going to do better than Randall. He's going to be a minister like his uncle. His people have connections, and he's got a good head on his shoulders."

Always ready to judge a book by its cover, Auntie Shirl continues to tick off Randall's qualities. She doesn't like Boone but I admire him. He is a real friend, and a good son and he's better than Randall Whitten in every way.

"I have some homework to do, Auntie Shirl," I say excusing myself from the table and heading toward my attic getaway. "I'll come down in a little while and clean up the kitchen."

"You're stubborn just like you father," she says as I climb the stairs.

I put my textbook into the box next to my bed and retrieve a *Life* magazine. Auntie Shirl is right about one thing, I really do love magazines. I have become a regular at the five-and-dime where I sometimes spend up to an hour deciding which one to purchase for the week.

Mr. Grayson used to greet me when I arrived at his store, but that changed after an incident in early November. A young, colored boy ran into the drugstore while I was considering the magazine display. He was out of breath and in a hurry. "Please sir, I need some soda powder," he had said loudly to Mr. Grayson and waved a scrap of paper. But Mr. Grayson took offense. "What's that you say, boy? Don't come running in here hollering. I've told you boys before this is a respectable place of business and I'm not going to stand for no nigger foolishness." The boy couldn't have been more than eight years old and began crying, so I tried to help. I took the paper from his hand.

"Mr. Grayson, the paper says he needs some bicarbonate of soda. Is that right young man?" The boy was sobbing and his nose was running.

"My mama's sick. Her stomach hurt and she can't breathe," he managed to say.

Grayson snatched the paper from my hand, and mumbled as he scooped a small amount of the powder into a brown paper cone. Then a white woman came into the drugstore and he turned his attention to her, so I took the boy's nickel from his hand, and slapped it firmly on the counter. Grayson glared at me, and handed the medicine to the boy who ran from the drugstore without another word.

Mr. Grayson and I hadn't shared many words since, either.

I stop flipping pages in my magazine to read a caption below a photograph. It is of an army infantry division in Palermo. The photo is like the one in the army recruitment office in Florence where I enlisted in the WAACS.

Enlisting had been a lot like college registration. "What's your name and your place of birth, young lady?" the recruiter had asked. It was the first time I'd had a real conversation with a young, white man. I thought he looked very sharp in his khaki shirt and brown slacks, and he was very helpful. He gave me a handful of forms and walked me to a table near the window. It took the better part of an hour to fill out all the forms, and I had to ask a couple of questions before it was all done. In only ten days I received my orders.

I pull the official letter from under the mattress of my bed and read it again. In a week I am to report to the bus station in Florence for the ride to Jacksonville, Florida where I will board a train for basic training. I am excited, and scared, and things are happening very fast.

Henrietta shook her head in disbelief when I told her what I'd done. "Won't your mama kill you when she finds out?' she asked with real concern. 'Girl, what you gonna' do?'

I know what I have to do. I must go home to face mama and daddy. They will be disappointed that I'm not staying at Linwood, and daddy will think I am unappreciative. But I'll simply have to face their disappointment. I've already notified

65

the registrar's office I am leaving school, I've quit my job at the cafeteria, and most of my things are packed.

I return downstairs to tell my aunt that I am leaving for home tomorrow morning. She is already washing the dishes, so I pick up a dish towel to dry. When I tell her I have joined the army, she is a lot angrier than I imagined.

"Young lady, you are too independent for your own good. Just think what this will do to your mother. Georgette Lillian Newton, are you listening to me?"

"I'm sorry Auntie," I say, and put down the dish towel.

"I promised your mama I would help you make a go of it at Linwood. You are doing well at school and you've met new friends, but now you're ready to leave. You've been here only a few months."

"Linwood is a fine school. It's just not what I want."

"What *do* you want, girl? How many colored folks do you see in those magazines you always have your nose in? That's not the world you live in. You have to know your own place."

"But things are changing, Auntie. The war is opening up doors for us. We don't have to settle for the way things used to be."

"You're naïve girl. Things haven't changed that much, I can tell you that. Your uncle thought joining the union would make things better. But you can't make white people respect you because you join a union, or because we're at war. People

66

are going to be who they are. Your life is better than most colored girls your age, why can't you be satisfied with what you have? I just don't understand you, Georgette."

And you never will, I think to myself before I go upstairs to finish packing.

Auntie Shirl does not speak to me when I leave her house early the next morning, but I know she will call mama as soon as she can.

I arrive in Pender right after noon and I walk the three miles to the farm. It is Saturday, not very cold, and little wisps of clouds stretch like skeleton fingers across the turquoise sky. The walk has helped me clear my head, and settle the butterflies in my stomach, and I've practiced the words I will say to my parents.

I stand at the road for a few minutes looking at our house. Mama and my sisters are probably out back washing clothes, and hanging them to dry on the clothes lines that crisscross one area of our rear yard. Daddy is not far away because his truck, with the hood up, is at the side of the house. I let myself in the front door and place my suitcase and box against the wall. The scent of some kind of roasting meat drifts from the kitchen, and I recognize the distinct aroma of rutabaga. Our old calico, Ginger, comes from another part of the house to investigate the opening of the door and rubs against my leg in greeting. When I bend to return the rub she turns, her tail high in the air, and walks away nonchalantly. My 'hello' is done.

I hear my sisters making the noises associated with their chores. There are giggles, and the scrape of washtubs along the floor of the wood porch as they hand wash sheets, pillow cases, daddy's shirts and coveralls, as well as their own dresses, nightgowns, and the family's undergarments. Since I've been away the supervision of this work must have fallen to Barbara because she yells to Ruthie to be careful not to drop clothes on the ground. I imagine her straining to turn the handle of the clothes wringer, drawing water from the sheets while keeping an eye on the other work. I am only a few steps into the front room, still taking in the familiar sounds and smells of home when I am startled by my mother's voice.

"You look as if you've lost more weight."

"Mama, I didn't see you there."

She sits in the afternoon shadows of our dining room in one of the plastic-covered chairs we have had since I was a child.

"Your father is furious with you, Sis."

"I know you must be disappointed, mama. I just wanted to come home to see you and daddy and the girls before I go." It's what I've practiced saying but the tears forming in my eyes are unexpected.

"I *am* disappointed, but not really surprised. I've been anticipating this ever since your birthday in October, but I'd hoped you would call me to talk it over one more time."

I remain in the middle of the room. There seems too much distance between my mother and me, to approach her. The awkward silence stretches out until Helen darts in through the back door calling to mama that there is still enough water in the basin to wash the bedroom rugs. She sees me when she enters the dining room.

"Sis, you've come back! Sis is here, Sis is here!" Helen screams toward the window to Barbara and Ruthie, and flings herself into my embrace. "I miss you so much," she sobs into my shoulder.

My other sisters come running, and Mama rises from her chair leaving us four girls to hug and kiss.

"Why didn't you tell us you were coming home today?" Barbara asks.

"What did you bring me?" shouts Ruthie over the voices of the others.

By this time we are in a circle with hands clasped. Then daddy opens the front door. His silhouette fills the threshold, and our celebration ceases immediately. There is something uneasy in his stillness and I'm glad I can't see his face.

Mama hurries in from the kitchen. "Girls, you better get back to the washing. It will be dark soon enough and all those

69

clothes need to be hung on the line, and the basin and wringer need to be stored away and the porch mopped dry."

Slowly, Barbara, Helen and Ruthie pull away from me, our hands untangling, as they return to their chores.

"George," mama says moving past me to close the front door and turn on the table lamp, "Sis has come home...for a visit."

Daddy looks at me, and then to mama. "When will supper be ready?"

"At the usual time," she replies.

"I guess you think you're grown now?" he asks without looking my way.

"No sir."

"Well then, maybe you can go and help your sisters finish the wash."

"Yes daddy."

"Your mama and I will talk to you after supper."

Daddy goes into the bedroom closing the door behind him. Mama gives me a look of support and her hand brushes my arm as I move to the back porch.

Supper is pleasant enough. I have missed mama's good cooking. Auntie Shirl can't equal my mother's magic in the kitchen. Daddy talks about the black newspapers' 'Double V' campaign. He tells us colored soldiers are resentful about their time in the service because they are still being treated like second-class citizens. When he remembers my situation he ducks his head, clears his throat, and changes the subject.

"Susie, I think we're going to need a new truck pretty soon. I spent most of the day again trying to fix that damn transmission."

"George, please watch your language." Daddy ducks his head for the second time in half a minute.

"I was hoping we might be able to buy one of those new wringer washing machines this winter," Mama says. "It takes the girls almost half the day to do laundry."

"Oh, we don't mind doing the wash, mama," Helen offers sincerely. She really is a sweet girl, content to be on the farm and with her life.

"I know dear, but you also have lots of other chores and I'm sure you girls wouldn't mind having time to spend with your friends on Saturdays every now and again."

"Now that Sis is back maybe she can help us with the wash, mama," Ruthie pipes in wanting to be a part of the conversation.

This sends our meal into an uncomfortable quiet until Ruthie parrots: "I'm sorry, I should only speak when I'm spoken to."

"It's okay Ruthie," I say. "I *am* going to help around the house until I have to leave."

My father and I peer at each other across the table.

"Who wants some banana pudding?" Mama says.

After supper daddy goes out back to smoke. He sits on the tree bench I helped him build when I was nine years old. I remember that afternoon so clearly. He made a little drawing of how the bench would look, then showed it to me because I was his helper. He sawed six long pieces of lumber into several smaller pieces. I held a clump of nails in my small palm, and my job was to hand a nail to daddy when he asked for it. He made a pencil mark in the wood, placed a nail on the mark then pounded it a couple of times until it took hold. "Okay baby, I need another one," he'd say and then place the nail I gave him between his lips while he hammered the first nail deep into the board. We worked like that for hours. "I'm helping, ain't I daddy?" I asked him a half dozen times. "Yes you are, Sis. I couldn't do it without you."

Even now, sitting on that bench gives you the feeling you are part of the maple tree it surrounds. The tree's vibrant red leaves have provided us shade every summer for as long as I can remember. Daddy loves that maple, and every inch of this land his family has owned for scores of years.

My sisters and I clear the table, put food scraps in a bucket for our nine hogs, prepare dish water, and put leftovers in the ice box. It's nice to be with my sisters, and even though we tease and laugh we work with precision and efficiency. Mama has taught us well. "Cleanliness is next to godliness," she often says. I pause from scrubbing pots when mama puts on her sweater and slips through the back door to join daddy. I watch through the kitchen window as she sits close to the man who has been her sweetheart since childhood. I excuse myself from the kitchen work and stand near the open dining room window to eavesdrop on their conversation.

"George, listen to me."

"I don't wanna hear it, Susie."

"I know Sis has a mind of her own...but she's a good girl. You know that."

"What's that got to do with anything?"

"She has always been a source of pride for us. We can't turn our back on her now or I think we could lose her."

Daddy is old fashioned when it comes to his wife and daughters, but he loves my mother above all things. He takes a long puff on his cigarette, drops it into the dirt, and grinds it with his boot. I smile when he puts his arm around mama and tells her what I have often heard him say: "You're right, Susie. You're always right as rain."

News travels like dandelion seeds on the wind in Pender. By the time the barber shop opens on Tuesday, everyone knows I'm home for a visit, and where I'm headed next. Boone comes

73

to the house to pick me up on my last day home and we walk to his house where we sit together on his front porch until dusk.

"You seem angry with me?"

"Am I supposed to be happy for you, Lil?"

"I wish you were. You know better than anyone why I'm joining the army."

We'd gone over it many times in the past, so we just hold hands and watch a few fireflies move playfully across the field next to his house. His mother brings out glasses of lemonade and visits for a while then Boone drives me home in his daddy's truck, but first we stop at one of the turnoffs between our two farms. He holds me close and we share long kisses. He moves his hand to my breast and the other touches my leg.

"Boone, you know better."

"I'm afraid I'm going to lose you. What if you meet someone, and just forget all about me?"

I answer him with the sweetest kiss I have to give.

Chapter 6

(Georgette)

I've been stationed at Ft. Huachuca for two weeks and have
the beginning of a new life. WAACS are an elite group and we
have a lot to prove to ourselves and to the army. It has taken an
act of Congress to allow only 150,000 women in the entire
country to serve. Our role is to take on tasks that will free up the
men to fight. Some of the girls complain about their new
routines: marching, studying, living with a bunch of other
women, and being away from family but each day I awake with
eagerness. In fact I feel a bit selfish when I think of the
opportunities this fight among nations has given me.

The women are assigned to barracks far away from the men,
but both groups are very aware of the other. Like the male
troops, the Negro and Caucasian WAACS sleep and eat in
separate facilities, but some of our work is done shoulder-to-
shoulder with our white counterparts. Our unit leader,
Lieutenant Charity Zanjeck, is Caucasian and one of a few
enlistees accepted into the officer's training school for women.
She grew up as an army brat so she understands base life and
army regulations. Her knowledge has helped us many times as
we adjust to a war-time army where women are a novelty.

"Where are you from, Newton?" she asks me during roll
call.

"Pender County in North Carolina, ma'am."

"I know Pender, that's not too far from Fort Bragg. You ever work tobacco, Newton?"

"Why, yes ma'am I have. My daddy grows a lot of tobacco."

"Well then I'll give you some advice. Army work is a lot like processing a tobacco crop. It takes a lot of people doing different parts of the job, but each part is dependent on the other. You have to do your part at the right time, and in the right way, so others can do their jobs well."

"Yes ma'am. I think I see what you mean."

I'm assigned to the personnel unit as a clerk. That's where I met Loretta and Clarice and we have become fast friends. There are about two dozen of us who type, code, and maintain the paperwork of nearly ten thousand soldiers at Ft. Huachuca. I like the variety. Sometimes I am in the personnel building all day, other times I transport files from one building to another. I have to coordinate with the hospital staff to update files about illnesses, injuries or service status. I even have the sad duty of adding certificates of death to the files of fallen soldiers then shipping those files off to the Department of the Army in Washington, DC. I don't think I'll ever get used to that.

WAACS are expected to stay fit and I spend many hours each week exercising and doing march drills. Our physical appearance also extends to our dress. We were issued two uniforms: a green, wool gabardine short jacket, straight skirt, brown shoes, stockings and a hobby hat for our dress uniform. The other, a khaki blouse with a dark-green skirt and belt, is my work attire. Only the girls assigned to maintenance, or who drive the supply trucks have permission to wear trousers. But regardless of rank or assignment there are a few articles of clothing we all have in common, the undergarments—they are itchy, and an ugly, drab-green.

My unit rises at 6 a.m. to shower and dress then we make up our cots and put away our personal items in trunks at the foot of our bunks. Once a week we have inspection, but this morning Lt. Zanjeck enters our barracks for a surprise inspection, accompanied by the base officer, Captain Hurley.

Hurley doesn't have a great reputation among the Negro soldiers. The seasoned troops say he resents being assigned to Huachuca where so many colored soldiers are stationed. He walks from cot to cot pretty quickly. He pauses at a few beds checking their tightness by bouncing a quarter off the blanket— so far, the inspection is perfect. He gives me a quick glance as he passes my bunk. When he returns to the front of the barracks he asks a question aloud.

"Does anyone here know what role you play in this man's Army?"

No one speaks up. Each of us knows we are doing jobs traditionally done by male soldiers so they can be free for combat duty, and that's what one of the girls finally says.

"Well that's why you were allowed to join the Army in the first place," Hurley says dismissing her answer. "But that's not your role."

Lt. Zanjeck stands very still, her eyes straight, as Hurley has his fun with us. I raise my hand and Hurley looks my way.

"Yes, Private?"

"Well, we each have a part to play to help the whole effort. If we do our small parts well the other bigger parts of the work will also go well." I stop, suddenly afraid I have said too much.

Hurley stares at me a moment.

"Very good, Zanjeck," Hurley says spinning on his heels and exiting the barracks.

The lieutenant smiles at me, and gives me a wink.

As agreed, I am sending a portion of my pay check to daddy for the money spent on college. I am happy to do it. I make more money than I have ever seen in my life, plus I get free meals and room and board. I proudly purchase a money order, write my father's name on it, and mail it from the PX. Daddy should have his money in a week and I'll send another check next month on my pay day. I am my own woman and it feels good.

On the walk back to my barracks, I pass through the recreation hall and see Private Dowdell sitting by himself and writing. I go out of my way to walk by his table but he doesn't even look up. His name is Leroy, and he's a friend of that fresh guy from Georgia they call Pit, but I want to know more about Leroy, so I stop off at the administration building and pull his file.

He's from Georgia, a high-school graduate, and only eighteen. On his aptitude tests he is average, but apparently he is an excellent musician. He lists his parents as 'living', with no siblings. He is five-foot-ten, and weighs 170 lbs. *That's perfect.* He isn't as tall as Boone, and he's younger than me, but he's quite attractive. He has a way of walking that is not in a hurry, and he isn't loud or immature acting like some of the other men, including his friend Pit. Out of curiosity I also look at Pit's file. His real name is Jerome Turner. He hasn't graduated from high school, and he is almost nineteen. The personnel form says 'unknown' under parents, and his last mailing address is The Brickstone Orphanage in Bluffton, Georgia.

"I thought you were off duty." I didn't hear Loretta come into the file room.

"I am."

"What are you looking at?" she asks.

"Oh, nothing," I say, closing the two files and adding them to the pile on my desk to be returned to their appropriate places. "Loretta, you like that Pit boy don't you?"

"Is that whose file you were reading?" Loretta asks.

My blush gives me away and I laugh. "Okay, I looked at Pit's file but I'm more interested in his friend, LeRoy."

"Yeah he's dreamy, but he's too quiet. Pit knows how to have a good time. He's going to escort me to church on Sunday and LeRoy is usually with him, do you want me to introduce you?"

"I'd like that."

"Well, consider it done."

Chapter 7

(LeRoy)

I hear daddy's moan. Trout's head, covered in blood, rests in his lap. The red spreads across his pants, reaches out to my hand and seeps through the straw turning it dark crimson. A shot rings out. I sit up straight in my bunk covering my ears. I am more than a thousand miles from that barn.

My shirt is soaked with sweat and I worry the beating of my heart will wake the guys around me so I lay back and take deep breaths until my heart slows. The nightmare has momentarily pulled me from the strangeness of the army, and sent me to the familiar strangeness of home. I've sent only one letter to my mother since I came to the base three months ago. In it, I told her of my daily life here and inquired about her health. I don't want to call home because my father answers the telephone and since we had so little to say to each other in person, I doubt we can carry on a long distance conversation.

I play out a tune in my head. It is a piece I've been working on since I arrived in Huachuca, and I plan to send it to Mr. Giles when it's finished. I imagine sitting in the horn section of a swing band in a crowded New York City nightclub wearing a red jacket, white slacks and brown saddle shoes. Couples glide across a polished ballroom floor keeping time with the beat. I stand for my solo, my trumpet pointed at the chandelier. I see the notes swirl up to the ceiling and the room becomes noisier as my playing excites the crowd. The other musicians signal their approval by tapping their feet, and the band leader smiles his admiration.

It's dark in the barracks and the snoring from forty soldiers begins to mix with the music. I make a hollow in my pillow with a couple of light punches, bury my head in it, and pull the scratchy wool blanket over my shoulders.

We are up early, 0600 hours on the dot. That's when Sergeant Moses slams into the barracks abruptly turning our sleep into the workday. Even in this dusty climate he is always what the army calls 'spit and polish'—the sand is also afraid to take him on.

He whacks the foot of our cots with a baton as he walks down the long aisle, and he makes a point of banging loudly on Pit's cot. "Get up, mama's boy," he often yells at Pit when jolting him from sleep.

"Hey man, Moses really has it in for you," one of the guys says to Pit in the shower.

"What did you ever do to him?" another guy asks.

"I didn't do a damn thing to him. He just don't like me." Pit shakes his head.

The first soldier offers his own opinion. "Maybe he's just an Uncle Tom, and wishes he was white."

"I wish he was white, too, so he could be on the other side of the base," the first guy says.

The two soldiers share a laugh. But, Pit isn't laughing. He has confessed to me that the thing he dreads most in the army is bedtime because he knows, with the light of day, his first sight will be the sneering face of Sergeant Moses.

Socializing between the races is frowned upon in the army so we usually keep to our own, but as the war takes more and more soldiers overseas, the brass at Huachuca decide on a single mess hall for all personnel. The rule is, however, that Negroes and whites will sit on opposite sides of the room. That's how were seated for breakfast.

Some of the white recruits are decent enough, and there is a guy from Mississippi who comes to our end of the dining hall from time to time to bum a Chesterfield. He says he likes some of us better than the stuck up white recruits from the North. Burt is well over six feet tall, and is the size of three of me. He has red hair that stands straight up like a brush and a handful of freckles dot both his cheeks. When he walks, he doesn't really lift his feet, he shoves them forward. I bet his mama had to get his shoes re-soled once a month when he was growing up.

"One of you boys got a smoke?" Big Burt asks our table.

"Boy, why don't you buy your own cigs sometimes," Pit teases. "You got more smoke puffing out of you than them freight trains we unload."

Burt joins in the laughter while he waits for his cigarette, but tones it down when he notices the looks he gets from the other side of the room. He takes his Chesterfield, nods his thanks, and shuffles back to his own people. That's just the way things work at Huachuca.

After breakfast we stand in line for our work assignment. Each day is the same. We shower, we shave, we dress, we make up our cots, we stand in line, we eat, we march, and we dig holes. A lot of holes—for building foundations, drainage ditches, to bury garbage, and to fill with gravel for new roads. Pit is always complaining he doesn't see much difference between a soldier's work and the work he had back home.

But today we have a change in our routine. Moses orders us to fall out. "Report to the south exercise field for weapons training," he growls. "Two by two, on the double, hut!"

We run double-time to the exercise field, which is up the hill a half mile past the holes we dug a month ago for the new latrines. Pit and I run together.

"Man, finally!" he says. "We get to hold some guns instead of them damn shovels. You know what I mean, LeRoy?"

I'm panting, and have to work a bit to keep up with Pit. He is in top physical shape.

"I was wondering when we was going to learn how to kill us some Germans," Pit continues. "I was beginning to think the plan was to win this war by having them sauerkrauts fall into the holes we been digging." He flashes a wide grin, his arms pumping as we run.

"No talking," barks Sergeant Moses.

Out of the corner of my eye, I see Moses watching Pit and me as he keeps pace with the unit. When we reach the south field, he orders: "Detail, halt. Left, face." We square up our line as we have been taught—holding out our right arms and pushing off the man next to us until our fingertips just brush against his shoulder.

The south field is one of the most isolated spots on base. Targets, in the shape of a man's head and torso, are set along the wire fence with nothing but miles of desert behind them. Bullets that don't hit their target can do very little damage here unless you're an unlucky jack rabbit or rattlesnake.

"Ten Hut."

We snap to attention. Our eyes forward, feet parallel, our hips tucked, and backs straight. Another sergeant approaches us.

"What have we here, Moses, another group of Bamas?"

Sergeant, Louis McCarthy's shirt is stretched tight across his gut. Only large amounts of beer, and fatty food everyday can get a belly that big. Sweat stains form dark patches at his armpits, and a semicircle of dampness shows where his stomach

85

meets the flab of his breasts. It's clear *he* isn't digging any holes. Moses gives the sergeant an ugly stare.

"They're as good as any men you've seen, McCarthy. I bet they'll show you a few things." Moses' words stun us.

"Well, I think they should still be swinging those shovels. It's a waste of time to issue rifles to this bunch of..." The white sergeant stops his name calling when he sees the hard set of Moses' jaw.

"Where do my men line up for their rifles, McCarthy?"

"At the supply station."

"About face," Moses orders giving a final, drop-dead look to the fat sergeant. "Forward, march," Moses says.

We are solemn. It doesn't escape any of us that for the first time Moses has called us men, and on top of that we are about to receive weapons.

"Dowdell," the clerk shouts, and I step up to the counter. The man pushes forward a paper. "Sign here for your rifle, boy." I don't mind the word 'boy' this time because it can't compete with the pride I feel as I hold an M-1 Garand automatic rifle. It's heavy, and the polished wood on the butt has the shine and color of one of the pipes Mr. Giles smokes.

It's only the second time I've held a gun. The first, was when I was eleven with my cousin's old single barrel shotgun. I fired it once, missing the wild turkey I'd taken aim at, and falling backwards from the recoil.

Self-consciously I look around to see if the other guys are stroking their rifles, as I'm doing. I can see they are as proud of the moment as me. There is a different set to our shoulders as we march to the target range. We finally feel like real soldiers.

Chapter 8

(Sgt. Moses)

Monday, 20 December 1943

Dear Bonnie:

I will call you Christmas morning and wish you the season's best but I am thinking of you tonight and my loneliness and despair compels me to reach out to you. I hope this letter finds you better than I.

It is relatively quiet these days at Huachuca. Nearly a third of the soldiers on base have gone home on a rare holiday furlough, and it could be the last time they will see their families in a long while. The war is intensifying in Italy and rumors are flying that even some of our boys may be deployed to the European theatre. Most of the colored troops, even some of the women, are itching to get to the fight, and I pray they will have the chance.

It's a very difficult time for me now. You know I love the army, but I have a burden that is hard to bear. Our Negro troops, regardless of rank or commitment, continue to be treated as second-class soldiers. I must plead and cajole for every opportunity that would prepare my recruits for combat. Although I fear very few of them will ever get overseas, let alone see the front lines. Today, B Company was issued rifles and the paperwork and politics required to provide these soldiers with the simple tools of their trade was unfitting. Yet, I would do it all again to witness the change in these boys when they received their own weapons.

The recruits coming to us two years into the war are rough boys just off the farm, unsophisticated and way out of their league. Some have potential to be good soldiers. They lack only training and, more importantly, hope. If they could believe they will be given an equal chance to perform as American soldiers, many would prove themselves worthy of the uniform. I won't be a nursemaid to these boys; that is not my style. So I try to set an example by my own demeanor and resolve. I'm tough on these recruits because I want them to be ready if they ever do face a real combat situation, but they seem to misunderstand my efforts and I believe I am failing them.

Every day, I battle within myself not to hit some redneck who insults me. I am a better soldier than any of the white noncoms and I know my love of country is equal to theirs, but they look past my uniform and only at my color. It's not just me. There are a dozen Negro officers on base who must feel heaviness even greater than mine. Protocol won't allow them to discuss it with me, but I can see it in their eyes when their repeated requests for overseas assignments for their squads are summarily dismissed.

Still, the most painful looks come from the troops themselves when I order them to some menial task that has nothing to do with fighting for the freedom of our country and of our allies. A lot of these young guys signed up expecting there would be glory in being an American soldier or, at the very least, respect. Neither is afforded them on this desert outpost.

I've burdened you enough with my complaints, sweet Bonnie. I know you have your own difficulties with the care of your dear mother, and the distance from all that you love (and I hope that includes me). I miss the feel of you under my body, the smell of your skin, and the sound of your laughter. I love you.

There. I've said it, and it gives me a release you cannot imagine. There is no one else to whom I can confide my deepest longings.

With all affection I remain, your Robert.

The tavern staff has begun to stack the chairs. I fold, seal and address my letter, and drain the rest of the bourbon in my glass. I can hear Bonnie's admonishment not to drink too much, but it really is the only thing that gives me solace.

Chapter 9

(Georgette)

It's the first Christmas I've been away from my family. I
don't have much time to feel sorry for myself, but the letter I
received from Barbara makes me a bit homesick. She writes
that daddy has completed decorating our house with pine boughs
and an eight foot tree he cut from our stand of pines in the north
orchard. Barbara says the tree gives the whole house a rich,
woodsy smell. Mama and the girls have been baking maple
syrup, walnut cookies for a week, and delivering them to our
neighbors and church friends. Ruthie has a role in the school
Christmas pageant playing a shepherd. Mama has made her a
costume from an old sheet and a tablecloth.

"Got a letter from home, Newton?"

Lt. Zanjeck is approaching my desk.

"Yes ma'am." I say hurriedly pushing the letter aside, and
standing up to greet an officer.

"At ease, Newton," Zanjeck says and sits at my side chair.
"You can sit down too, Newton. I just stopped by to see how
you're doing. It's tough to be away from home at holiday time
isn't it?"

"Yes ma'am. It is," I admit.

"But it's a choice we make when we sign up. My sister and her family are celebrating Christmas with my mother. They all live in North Carolina, near the mountains. It's beautiful there this time of year."

"Yes ma'am. Mama says they're expecting snow for Christmas in Pender. It doesn't happen that often, but when it does, our farm looks like one of those covers on the *Saturday Evening Post.*"

Lt. Zanjeck looks at me and laughs.

"What made you sign up, Newton?"

The question surprises me and I don't know where to start. "Well…I'd been thinking about it for a long time."

"I bet your family wasn't too pleased."

"No ma'am. Not at all," I shake my head remembering.

Lt. Zanjeck nods. She's an attractive woman, tall with blond hair, a strong jaw and clear blue eyes the color of a lake— she sort of reminds me of Marlene Dietrich. I feel comfortable telling her about the reactions back home to my joining the WAACS, my brief stay at college, and how I'm sure I've made the right decision.

"It's a new time for women," the lieutenant says. "The country had no choice but to let us try things we've always wanted to do; things that didn't fit the rules somebody else had made for us. My father used to say, a war tests countries and families."

"Was your father always a soldier?" I ask.

"As far back as I can remember, and my mother was a soldier's wife. We traveled all over the world and I went to school in six different countries. I have a brother and a sister, but I'm the only one who wanted to be a soldier, like my dad."

We all knew Lt. Zanjeck's father died in the Solomon Islands a year ago. He was a Colonel, a decorated hero, and could have stayed safely in Washington, DC, but after Pearl Harbor he'd asked to be sent to the front lines.

"My father is a farmer and I think that's all he's ever wanted to be. There are four girls in my family, and I'm the oldest. I think if I were a boy he would be proud of me, but he's an old fashioned man, and wants me to be the way daughters are supposed to be."

"What about your mother?" Zanjeck asks.

I smile at the thought of mama. "I really think she would make a good soldier. She's capable of most anything, and is a natural born leader. You should see how she gets my father to do anything she wants him to do."

We share a laugh.

I admire Lt. Zanjeck. Women in the army is a new thing and a lot of people are waiting for us to fail. If we mess up at Ft. Huachuca, she'll be blamed. It's clear she's under a lot of scrutiny, but she's always very professional and respectful of us as women, and soldiers.

"Well, I can tell you one thing, Newton," Zanjeck says as she stands to leave, and I also stand as protocol requires. "Your mother *and* father should be very proud of you. You are doing a fine job, and you're just the kind of young lady we hoped would join the WAACS."

Loretta, Clarice and I prepare to attend a Christmas party and dance, sponsored by the local Negro civic association which will be held tonight in the basement of the All Saints Baptist church in Tucson. The invitation was extended by the church's pastor and his wife during a recent Sunday service. The women of the congregation will cook us a wonderful meal of the things we know and love. Of course, there will be no alcoholic beverages but the reverend promised us lots of fresh lemonade and iced tea sweetened with cane sugar. The home-cooked food will certainly be a treat, but it's really the dance everyone's excited about.

"I sure hope Pit likes my hair," Loretta shrills as she pins up her French roll. She is slightly plump, with curves in all the right places, and a gold complexion that drives the men wild.

"I don't know why you even bother primping," Clarice says. "You know that dumb fool is always grinning from ear to ear when he's around you."

Pit is very sweet on Loretta. When he sees her at the recreation hall, he abandons his buddies to sit next to her, and usually escorts her to services at the chapel. Often he brings along his good-looking friend. I see LeRoy all the time on work detail, doing rifle drills, or just walking around the base and he will nod if Pit calls out a greeting, but so far he has given me no reason to think he takes any special notice of me. He is a quiet guy...not really free and easy like Pit, or some of the other fresh boys who constantly flirt with me. The girls at the base post office, say he gets a lot of letters and postcards from home from his mother, and from one of his teachers. He plays clarinet and trumpet in the Negro band on base, and by all accounts is a top-notch musician. When the guys go to town for movies or a beer, LeRoy usually skips the beer for a visit to the local music store to listen to records, and buy sheet music and reeds for his clarinet.

"Georgette, are you day dreaming about LeRoy again?" Clarice teases. "You got that look on your face, like when you're reading one of them magazines of yours."

I had to laugh at myself. I didn't realize I'd stopped fixing my hair, and was staring into the mirror. Loretta and Clarice are almost ready, so I quickly brush the coarse hair at the base of my neck. At home we call that part of the hair, 'the kitchen' and I've never known why. I put on gold clip-on earrings, and apply plum-colored rouge to my lips, and blend a dab on both cheeks.

Lip rouge is hard to come by in war time, and we can't wear makeup while on duty, but tonight we are all dolled up, and feel glamorous.

The three of us leave the barracks in good spirits. We turn up the collars of our coats to protect us from the night air, and join one of the cheerful groups heading to the buses that will take us on the one-hour drive into Tucson. The time passes easily as we flirt with the boys, and they with us. Those who are already sweethearts, snuggle close together in the cover of the bus shadows. I look around for LeRoy, but he must be on one of the other buses.

The dim outline of the Huachuca Mountains looms in the distance, under a sky filled with stars and a half moon. This remote base is a continent away from the war, and a world away from our old lives. A baritone voice starts up, 'Silent night, Holy night' and others pick up the tune. From the darkness comes the nasally sound of a trumpet mouthpiece, and I turn towards the back of the bus as others do. I can just make out LeRoy's profile against the moonlit rear window, his head bobbing up and down as he lends his soul to our melody. The first night of the Christ child must have been much like this— still and cold, under a vast, star-filled sky. When the song ends, the bus falls quiet for only a few moments, before someone picks up the next song. "Oh come all ye faithful," the voices ring out.

Chapter 10

(LeRoy/Georgette)

The church basement has two large rooms all decked out for the holidays. Thirty, round tables have centerpieces of Poinsettia, atop bright-red tablecloths. Multi-colored lights are strung around the basement's pillars. A record player sits on top of an elevated stage, and Christmas music swells through the room. The food is a feast fit for the occasion, and has been prepared by the ladies of the church with the care and attention given to the meals they cook for their own families. They stand behind serving tables, some wearing their Sunday hats, and ladle butter beans and collard greens, roast turkey and yams, cornbread dressing, pork loin, green peas, homemade rolls, and even two huge pots of chitlins.

Pit and I sit with Loretta and her friends, Clarice and Georgette. I've noticed Georgette looking at me from time to time, and when I got off the bus tonight she told me how much she liked my playing on *Silent Night*. She's a cute girl with brown skin, flashing eyes and a very sweet smile, but it is her voice I like most. When she says my name, it rolls slowly over her tongue and on 'roy', her voice goes up an octave.

She keeps looking my way, and I want to make small talk, but so far I haven't thought of anything that doesn't sound dumb. I'm not good at talking to women, not like Pit who can just walk up to any girl and strike up a conversation. "You got to loosen up, LeRoy," he always scolds me, "and don't be looking so serious, you'll scare the women away."

In fact, I have very little experience with women. Back home, I took a couple of girls to school dances but those weren't really dates and I've never had relations with a girl. If the others found out, I would be teased without mercy. Fortunately there are several guys in our unit, including Pit, who are eager to talk about their own romantic skills, so I can just nod and smile, pretending I know what they're talking about.

When we finish eating, Pit gets up and moves his chair next to Loretta, and Clarice joins a group near the stage who are examining the phonograph records we have for dancing. I brought six records: an Ella Fitzgerald, two by Louis Armstrong, a Benny Goodman song, and two Jimmy Dorsey selections. A couple of guys start stacking chairs and pushing tables to the side walls and someone replaces the Christmas song that was playing, with a swing record. Two couples take to the floor immediately with a jitterbug, and their hips and feet never stop moving. The male dancer is very tall, and when his partner shimmies low to the floor he throws a long leg over her head, lifts her up in a move called the bucking horse, and returns her gently to the floor.

I catch Georgette staring at me, again. But this time neither of us looks away. She smiles and I smile back.

"You want me to get you a piece of cake, LeRoy?" Georgette asks with musical notes.

"Uh, I wouldn't mind a piece of cake. I'll go with you so we can bring back some lemonade, too."

We stroll across the room together. I've gained weight and muscle during my four months at Huachuca, and my shoulders fill out the olive shirt that is neatly tucked in my dress trousers. I have a fresh haircut, and my tanned leather shoes are polished to a shine. Georgette is wearing her moss-green service jacket and skirt, and it shows off her shapely legs. At five-foot-five in her low-heeled shoes, her head reaches just above my elbow.

"Do you want Lemonade or sweet tea, Georgie?" I have decided that name fits her better than Georgette.

"Lemonade, for me," she says.

Her soft, black hair is worn loose. Normally, it is pinned up under her Hobby, but tonight it frames her face in a way that really shows off her freckled skin and her deep, brown eyes.

The church ladies at the dessert table smile as they cut cake and pour our beverages. "Here you are young man," one of them says handing us cups and plates. "I hope you and your young lady are having a good time."

I look over to see Georgette blushing, and I have to clear my throat before I can say, "Yes ma'am, we sure are."

I'm balancing two cups of lemonade in each hand as we weave through the crowd back to our table. Georgette walks a bit ahead of me holding plates with several pieces of cake and some cookies. Her hips swivel as she walks, and I notice a few guys gawking at her when we pass.

"Oh you're the man," Pit shouts when we return with the goodies. Georgette shares a look with Clarice who has returned to our table, then passes around forks and napkins and quickly sits. I slide a cup of lemonade across the table to her, and for a moment our fingers touch. I watch as she eats, and it is as if I am seeing her for the first time. She takes dainty bites, wiping her mouth often with her napkin. She knows I am looking, and bobs her head up between bites of cake to smile. Clarice abruptly pushes her chair away from the table, stands and announces that the girls are going to the ladies' room. Georgette and Loretta seem somewhat surprised, but follow Clarice's lead. Pit and I watch them as they zigzag through the dancers to the far end of the room.

"Georgette looks good tonight, man," Pit says, and I agree. "So, what you gonna do about it?"

I hunch my shoulders.

"She really likes you, and you better lay claim to her soon, because a lot of guys have been checking her out."

"I know, Pit. I like her too. But I don't know what to say to her."

Pit is eager to give advice, and by the time the girls get back to the table we have a plan.

LeRoy keeps glancing at me. I guess it's only fair, since I've been sneaking peeks at him for weeks. I'm glad I paid extra attention to my hair and makeup tonight. The food at the Christmas party is delicious almost as good as mama's home cooking, but now that we've all had our fill, some of the guys and girls are eager to dance and the Christmas music has been replaced with bebop.

Loretta and Pit are sitting close, and making goo-goo eyes at each other, and Clarice is across the room, so I offer to get dessert for LeRoy, and to my surprise he offers to accompany me. I pretend not to notice the ogling of a group of soldiers when LeRoy and I walk across the room, but I can feel their eyes on my backside. I think we must look like a couple, because the ladies who serve us our cake kind of smile at us like they know a secret. Then LeRoy surprises me by calling me 'Georgie'. I'm not sure where he came up with that, but I like it. It sounds like a city girl's name.

Clarice shoots me a curious look when LeRoy and I return to the table, but no one else notices. Then before we can even finish our cake, she grabs my shoulder bag from the table, and pulls me and Loretta off to the ladies room.

"Girl, what's going on?" Clarice asks as we scoot around one of the dancing couples.

"What do you mean?"

"I see the way LeRoy is looking at you. What happened? Did you say something to him?"

"I didn't say anything except I like the way he plays music, we've just been making small talk. The only thing that happened, was the dessert ladies assumed LeRoy and I were going together, and I thought I would just die."

"I knew it. I knew it," Clarice repeats. "I could tell something was different. He keeps batting his eyes at you, and what did he call you...did he say Georgie?"

We arrive at the restroom and find a line of WAACS laughing, talking and waiting their turns for the commodes and the mirrors.

"I think he is so handsome," I blurt out before I can stop myself. I look around to see if anyone besides Clarice and Loretta has overheard, but the music is loud enough to keep our conversation private. Clarice's eyes widen and then close in a squint. We don't say much more, just inch forward in the line until Loretta is able to plant herself in front of one of the mirrors, and Clarice and I cram in next to her. I pat my makeup with a moistened sponge, and apply fresh lip rouge. All the while Clarice stares at me in the mirror.

When we return to the main room, the church ladies are cleaning the serving area, and packing up the extra food. The deacons, all wearing dark suits, are gathering at the back of the room. They are our chaperones, and their presence is a reminder

103

that we are in a church building, and expected to behave appropriately.

"Are you ready to cut a rug, ladies?" Pit asks before we can even sit.

"Sure," Loretta agrees, tossing her pocketbook on the table, and holding out her hand to Pit who willingly encloses it with his own.

"Come on you guys," Loretta hollers back at us, as she and Pit scamper to the dance floor.

LeRoy, Clarice and I watch the two of them glide to the music. It's no surprise they are both good dancers. A soldier comes over and asks Clarice to dance and she obliges. Everyone seems ready to work off all that delicious food.

"It's a real nice party isn't it?" LeRoy asks the question as he moves to sit next to me, catching me off guard. "It's really better than I thought it would be. I wasn't sure what to expect about the dancing part, you know? But when I heard we could bring our own records, I figured we could let our hair down a little," he is smiling.

He smells of aftershave lotion and I've never seen him this close before. It is always a mystery to me why God gives some men such beautiful eyebrows, and full eyelashes when women have to work so hard on theirs.

"Are you ready to dance, Georgie?"

I answer by standing up. He takes my hand and we make our way to the middle of the dance floor. LeRoy is a good dancer, I guess most musicians are. We move easily together to Ella Fitzgerald, Benny Goodman, and Nat Cole. When Louis Armstrong's 'I'm in the Mood for Love' begins, he hesitates a moment, then pulls me close to his chest, one hand giving me a light touch around the waist and the other wrapped tightly around my palm.

Part Two

February 1944

Chapter 11

(Georgette/LeRoy)

In the weeks following the holiday dance, LeRoy and I spend most of our free time together. We take long walks on the base, and sometimes share a soda at the recreation hall. I tell him all about my life in Pender, and he tells me about his folks and his life in Americus. LeRoy describes his father as a sullen man...distant and sometimes hurtful, but he dotes on his mother, and I can tell by the way he speaks of her she is full of life and warmth despite her illness. Over time, I learn that LeRoy can display the qualities of both his parents.

We have Sunday passes today, and after church LeRoy, Pit, Loretta and I go into town to see *Cabin in the Sky* with Lena Horne, Ethel Waters, Eddie Anderson and Louis Armstrong. It is a wonderful movie with something for everyone. It has music and dancing, and a story about good, evil and temptation. In the nightclub scenes, the women wear beautiful gowns and the men are dashing and handsome. I know LeRoy likes those scenes too, because of the bands and Louis Armstrong's trumpet playing, but I noticed he became anxious when the character played by Eddie Anderson was smitten with Lena Horne and ready to leave his wife played by Ethel Waters. During that scene, he pulled his hand away from me, and folded his arms tightly against his stomach.

On the bus ride back to base, Pit and Loretta move all the way to the back, and began necking immediately. After three weeks of dating, LeRoy and I are still at the one, good night kiss, and hand-holding stage, but I know there is a growing connection between us. We like a lot of the same things and can talk for hours and hours, but I'm ready to do more than talk. It's strange for me to be the one who wants to go farther than a good-night kiss, which was not the case with Boone. Maybe it's because I'm almost three years older than LeRoy.

"Georgie, what did you think of Satchmo? He can really blow, can't he?" LeRoy asks excitedly.

"Yes, he was good." I move closer to him, so that our hips touch but he doesn't react.

"There were some really great dancers, and did you see those threads? That's the way I want to be able to dress one day."

"Do you think I would look good in that gown Lena wore?" I ask.

"What?"

"Remember, when she sang that first song at the club, she had on this rhinestone dress. I guess you think she's beautiful, huh?"

"I never thought about it too much but, yeah, she's a looker alright."

Apparently, Lena poses less of a threat for me with LeRoy than she does with Boone.

"What did your girlfriend Barbara look like?"

"Why do you keep asking me about her?" LeRoy is irritated. "I told you we weren't serious, I just took her to a dance, and she isn't as pretty as you. Is that what you want to hear?"

"No, that's not it at all," I lie. "I just wonder what you like in a girl. Are you a leg man, like Pit?"

"I like girls with big, brown eyes and voices like honey, who are just over five feet tall," Leroy says teasingly.

I decide not to press my luck. I know LeRoy likes me, but he is real cool about it, maybe too cool. I've told him quite a lot about Boone but he never asks questions. I guess he just isn't the jealous type. I glance toward the back of the bus and wonder if LeRoy and I will ever share the kind of passion Pit and Loretta have for each other.

Georgie scoots over and I can feel her thigh against mine. She keeps looking back at Pit and Loretta, and I take a look too. They're so close together, I can't make out one from the other.

She asks me about Barbara again, and then seems to be mad, so I put my arm around her shoulder and, she melts into me. I lean down to kiss her, and her lips seem eager to meet mine. Despite what I've let the guys think, kissing is all we've done. After a few kisses, I want to talk again.

"When we get to New York City, we'll go to a club just like the one in the movie."

Georgie says nothing.

"And you know, I think one day I'll be playing in one of those clubs."

She still doesn't respond, and pulls away so I remove my arm and she pulls her coat tight across her body. We sit in silence for a few minutes. I can tell I'm in trouble.

"Is something wrong?"

"All you ever want to do is talk about music and movies. Don't you find me attractive, LeRoy?"

"You're beautiful, Georgie. Don't I always tell you?"

"Yes, you tell me but you don't act like you believe it."

Pit has been coaching me on what girls want to hear, and how they think. I search my memory for the best thing to say.

"Pit can't keep his hands off Loretta, and all we do is kiss," Georgie finally says.

"You mean you want to do more?"

"Well…no, but I want you to at least *try* to do more."

Pit says women are fickle, I guess he's right. I'm confused by what she says but I don't want her to be mad. So, I tug at the lapels of her overcoat pulling her close, and give her a wet kiss.

Chapter 12

(Georgette)

There is still an hour before lights out, when Loretta and I return to the barracks. LeRoy gave me the sweetest goodnight kiss, and told me he thought I was the best looking girl on the entire base. I know Pit has been giving LeRoy tips on how to be more of a ladies' man, because he bragged about it to Loretta but I accepted LeRoy's compliment hook, line and sinker.

Clarice is dying to know all about the movie but I leave that duty to Loretta because I want to get a letter written tonight, and get it in the post first thing tomorrow.

February 6, 1944

Dear Mama:

It is Sunday evening and as is so common, my thoughts drift to you and home. In my mind's eye I see you, daddy and the girls sitting around the table over dinner, with the curtains tied back to let in the soft light of the day's final hours. I know the house is filled with the aroma of baking bread, and the strong scent of the pine soap daddy lathers on after a day outdoors. I can hear Helen humming the tune she learned in glee club that she never tires of, and the soft murmur of your voice at bedtime prayers.

Tucson in winter is a drab place. Almost, every, day, the sun hangs high in a cloudless sky, but it offers little warmth, and the landscape has barely any color to illuminate. At night the sky is like a massive quilt of stars, but it is no comfort from a biting cold that makes the coyotes howl.

I miss you mama. I have good friends here, but none as wise as you, and not a week goes by that I don't wish I could pull you aside to talk through a problem, or share a new idea. I've been thinking a lot lately about the story of how you came to marry daddy instead of Uncle Butch. How daddy used to tag along when Uncle Butch came courting, until one day you realized it was daddy you really loved. I never thought to ask what it was about him that stole your heart, or whether he also knew he loved you. When I'm not on duty I have a lot of time to think about such things.

Well, I don't have much news to share since we last spoke. I went to the picture show with some friends tonight, and we saw *Cabin in the Sky*. It was fun to see the beautiful gowns, and dancing, and hear the music. I have been learning to drive a Jeep. My commanding officer, Lt. Zanjeck, says I am doing a very good job in all my work. Please let Daddy know that I have already sent him a money order for this month, and he should receive it next week.

I hope you are doing fine, mama, and that you don't worry about me too much. It is really a wonderful experience for me at Ft. Huachuca, and for everything I miss about Pender, there is something new to discover here. I try to read the papers every week—tell Daddy I guess the apple doesn't fall too far from the tree—and I have read about the good things Miss Eleanor Roosevelt is trying to do for Negro soldiers and for women. Next to you and Lt. Zanjeck, she is the woman I most admire. I think this terrible war will make things better for the Negro people all across America, and I hope I am doing my small part to help.

Well, that's all for now. Please give my love to daddy, Barbara, Helen and Ruthie and all my friends in Pender. I love you mama. I will call you next week. Sincerely, your daughter, Sis

There is now only fifteen minutes before the call for lights out, so I stuff the letter in an envelope, quickly address it and secure it in my handbag. Most of the girls are already in bed so I grab my pajamas and head to the latrine to change and brush my teeth. When I hop into my bunk I pull a magazine from under my pillow and

read a story about how Mrs. Roosevelt took the
opportunity to fly with one of the Tuskegee Airmen.

Chapter 13

(Sgt. Moses)

I had too much to drink last night. My aching head bears
the truth, and when I look in the mirror my face confirms it. My
eyes are puffy and my hands shake. It will be difficult to shave
this morning. I pride myself on my looks, I've been that way
since I was a boy growing up in Chicago's south side where
hygiene was less valued than one's prowess at fist fights. Most
of my hometown friends were petty criminals and ne'er-do-wells
who loved the street life, hated school, and never ventured very
far from our tough neighborhood. But, by the time I was
thirteen, I had a plan of escape. In high school, I pretended not
to care about learning while making sure I got passing grades. I
kept good standing with the guys by never backing away from a
fight, but I leaped at every opportunity to get exposure to people
and places away from my harsh life. I wore the brown suede cap
that symbolized my allegiance to my gang, but I also bought a
dress hat for the times I slipped off by myself to visit the art
museum. I became very good at this balancing act, fooling
everyone but my father.

"Why you shaving in the afternoon, boy?" he would ask
watching me from the bathroom door. "Where you going that
you can't stand to have a little stubble?"

I would try to play it off with some line like: "Dad, you know the girls like the feel of a smooth face."

He would look at me out of his runny, yellow eyes and suck his teeth. He didn't believe me, and I didn't give a damn that he didn't. He was an ignorant, volatile man, and this morning I look just like him.

My fourteen years in the Army have been a good fit for me. The pay is good, I have a position of responsibility, I've had opportunities for travel, and I don't have to explain my diligence for grooming. I keep my shoes polished, my nails and hair trimmed, and my uniform neat. While most of the other non-coms use the base laundry, I pay a woman in Tucson to starch and press my shirts. I have a thing about my shirts.

My mother took in laundry, and I learned from her how a well-laundered shirt should look and feel. I spent hours watching her hand wash and starch shirts, then hang them out to dry on a clothes line that she strung across the small, concrete balcony of our apartment. The arms and bodice of the shirts were stiff when she pulled them from the line, and she used an old milk bottle fitted with the head of a flower pot nozzle to sprinkle them with a light mist of water before rolling them, from the tail up to the collar, and tucking them into a towel-covered basket in preparation for pressing.

Ironing would take her all afternoon and continue after supper, and she explained each step to me as she worked. I helped by setting up her ironing board in the kitchen, and heating the iron on the stove top. The shirt collar, shoulders and sleeves were pressed first, and to protect the buttons from melting, she ironed the front of the shirt from the inside, carefully nosing the iron between the buttons.

"You see how I'm doing this, Robert?" she'd ask. "The pleats require a very hot iron."

She did this work, week after week, throughout my childhood and adolescence, and I witnessed her soft hands become dry and wrinkled from the starch, and her back more and more stooped, from lifting heavy baskets and bending over her ironing board.

I feel the nick of the razor, and snap my attention back to my shave. My eyes are judgmental, and I know it will be another trying day. Some of these young colored soldiers are an uncouth lot, like that Private Turner. They join the Army to escape hard work at home, or to sow wild oats away from their small towns, and they're surprised by the rules they have to follow here at Huachuca. A few will never cut the mustard, but I'll be damned if I let those honky sergeants make fools of these boys. That is the one thing about the Army I cannot abide. How, on the one hand, they promote a single standard of honor—loyalty to your fellow soldier and love of country—but apply a double standard when it comes to the treatment of its colored members.

That's why I have to be hard on somebody like Turner—the pride of our race is at stake. There is no room for shucking and jiving in these war times, we must be tough and ready to fight. That's what I learned on the south side of Chicago, and that's what I am going to hammer into these colored recruits, for their own, damned good.

A hundred of us sit in ten rows of folding chairs by rank and race. I sit in the last row trying not to concentrate on my throbbing head. This weekly briefing of Fort Huachuca's officers and non-coms is mandatory, including for the WAACs, and it's the only time we are all together.

Captain Hurley is commander of Huachuca, and he doesn't let anyone forget it. He's a pale man, thinly built with an enormous head that looks out of place on his narrow neck. Hurley is a career soldier who expected to be at a higher rank by now, and at a more prestigious post. It's common knowledge he is dissatisfied with his command at this out-of-the way military base.

He presides at a long table in the front of the room flanked by two other Captains twice his size. Behind him are a series of maps, one a detailed overhead view of Fort Huachuca, another of the surrounding territory including Tucson and the Mexican border, and there are several, large, color maps showing the European and Asian war theaters.

"Another two thousand soldiers will be leaving Huachuca at the end of the week," Hurley announces this morning. "This includes Companies sixteen, eighteen, twenty-one, twenty-four, twenty-seven, twenty-eight, thirty-one, and Negro Company twelve. These companies will ship off to Italy, those of you affected, should stay after this briefing to get details of your deployment."

A murmur goes through the room. Everyone is itching to get into the fight. Those of us who don't have troops shipping off, are angry because there is no glory in being left behind. One of the eight Negro lieutenants on base, raises his hand and Hurley acknowledges him.

"Sir, I'm proud that Company twelve is getting an overseas assignment. Do you have any sense of when some of the other Negro troops might be deployed?" Lieutenant Harry Wilson asks.

Moans begin among the white officers, and Hurley quiets them.

"What seems to be the problem, Wilson?" Hurley asks in a patronizing tone. "Don't your soldiers like it here?"

The white officers laugh, but   Wilson doesn't shirk.

"Captain, our men want to fight. Some of them have been at Huachuca for more than a year. They want to get some action, so they can tell their families what they're doing in the war."

"Are you telling me how to run this base, Lieutenant Wilson?" Hurley asks.

"Absolutely not sir, I just want to be able to give a report to the men that will keep up their morale, that's all it is, Captain,"

Wilson begins to feel the intimidation.

"What's wrong with their morale, Wilson?"

All of us in the last two rows shift in our chairs, when dozens of white faces turn toward the back of the room. We wonder if Wilson is prepared to speak the truth everyone, including Hurley, knows.

"Nothing is wrong with morale. My troops are performing their duties as required. They just hope they get a chance to show what they can do on the front lines." Wilson sinks to his seat, not willing to go further and put his army career in jeopardy.

"And I hope you continue to keep your men in line, Wilson. That goes for all of you," Hurley scans the back of the room. "Remember we all have roles to play."

"Sir?" Lieutenant Zanjeck raises her hand.

"What is it Zanjeck?"

"I just want to say a lot of the women feel the same way, colored and white," she turns sideways to acknowledge

120

Lieutenant Wilson. "They are performing at high, professional levels, and hope they will have a chance to serve overseas to have even more impact in supporting our fighting men."

Hurley stares at Zanjeck for a long time without speaking. She continues to stand, waiting for a response. Someone coughs, the hum of the air conditioning grows louder. We all know Zanjeck's deceased father affords her consideration she might not otherwise get. I've heard she uses it to her advantage on occasion.

"I appreciate your perspective, Lieutenant. Maybe we can discuss this in more detail in my office."

"Thank you, sir. I'll be sure to call your office for an appointment this week," Zanjeck says not letting Hurley off the hook.

"Of course," Hurley says and dismisses the meeting.

I notice Lieutenants Wilson and Zanjeck share a nod before they leave.

Chapter 14

(LeRoy)

Eight months have passed since I joined the army, and I
don't think I will ever get away from this desert. The white
soldiers get eight weeks of basic training then ship off overseas,
or to permanent duty somewhere else, but most of our troops
come to Fort Huachuca and never leave.

Occasionally my company receives weapons training and
that lifts our spirits, but most days we don't even pick up our
weapons except to clean them after doing a day's labor that has
little to do with being a fighting soldier. We drill for fires and
evacuations, work guard duty, unload supplies and do
maintenance. I am luckier than most, because at least I get a few
hours a week to practice with the colored marching band. But a
half-day of playing music, isn't going to help me become a
professional musician.

"Private Dowdell, you seem to have your mind elsewhere
today?" Sergeant Moses' voice is close to my ear.

"Uh, no sergeant," I stammer.

Today, my work detail is painting the exterior walls of the
north barracks. The other guys have already moved to the side of
the building.

"Well you've painted that one window for almost twenty minutes, and you're not done. Get a move on, soldier," he shouts leaning close to my face.

I dab my drying brush into the grey paint, and quickly finish the window frame then join the rest of the group. It seems to me, Sgt. Moses is directing a lot more attention my way than he has before. Maybe it's because I'm friends with Pit, who he still rides hard any chance he gets. This morning he made a point of giving Pit a job with the quartermaster detail, rather than the easier painting work, which means Pit is spending the day unloading supply trucks—tough work, made tougher by the sun.

"That son of a bitch," Pit whispered to me before heading off to his assignment. "One of these days, I'm really going to fix him."

The guys are stacking buckets of paint onto the truck to head to the next group of buildings, and I'm still working on the side door trim. I'm feeling so restless that it's hard to focus. I take a step back to check the paint job on the screen door, and it looks pretty good. I drop my brush in the empty bucket, put the top back on the 5-gallon paint container and grab both to put in the truck. Moses is watching me again. Damn, why is he all over me?

The sun blares like a sassy trumpet. The heat is very different from the stickiness of Georgia. My lips are parched, my muscles feel tight, and if I don't remember to drink lots of water, I'll get a leg cramp.

We're digging holes again today, this time at an excavation site on the far side of the base. I'm grateful when we break for lunch, but the meal hour passes quickly, and Pit, Sylvester, Bennie and I, slowly make our way back to our work site. We walk about a quarter of a mile on the dusty path, when we notice four white soldiers are following us. We turn to face them.

"Hey, you niggers, we just came out to inspect your work on our new movie hall," one of them says.

It's true, the earth we've moved all morning is for the foundation of a new recreation building for the white soldiers. The facility will have a swimming pool and a gymnasium. Our rec hall is an old airplane hangar, with a few game tables and a juke box. The windows are screenless, and there is no indoor plumbing. We turn away from the white soldiers and keep walking. It's too damn hot to fight.

"Hey, you nigger... Mr. Horn Player. I hear you're pretty good with that trumpet," the same soldier calls out to me. "But I bet you swing that shovel, better than you swing that horn."

The insult triggers laughter from his buddies.

"Don't pay any attention to them, Leroy," Bennie says tugging at my arm.

"I hear you boys might take your shovels overseas to help dig latrines, or maybe dig graves for some of them other coons

124

they're sending to the front lines." There is more laughing from the white soldiers, but this time Sylvester fires back.

"Maybe I'll put one of these shovels upside your big, pink, head."

There is but a single, breathless moment separating Sylvester's threat, from the first blow, as both groups charge the other. I see the mouthy white private double over from Sylvester's powerful fist to his gut. Pit lowers his head and dives into the fight, his arms stretched wide. Someone grabs my arm, and a fist glances off my jaw. I swing back stinging my knuckles as bone strikes bone. Bennie cusses under his breath, boots scrapes in the dirt and I hear grunts, from blows given and received, but otherwise there is little noise. I trip and fall backwards onto the sand and then see stars when a boot comes down hard on my eye. On the second kick, I roll away but my body seems to move in slow motion.

I'm not clear what happens next, but there is the sound of an angry voice and cracking wood. I am flat on my back, and a window shade has been pulled over half of the sun. Then I see a part of Sgt. Moses' face hovering over me. He barks orders, and Sylvester, Bennie and the white soldiers take off running in different directions. "Get Dowdell into the barracks, Turner," the Sarge shouts to Pit.

"Man, quick get inside."

Pit's tone is urgent as he pushes me inside the barracks door. I hold my head, it feels like it might explode, and blood spills through my fingers. The men who have cleaned our sleeping quarters are long gone, and my blood soils the floor as Pit pushes, and sometimes pulls me, pass the rows of cots and into the latrine where I fall in a heap on the tiled floor. Pit grabs a couple of towels, wets them with cold water, and presses them tightly against my forehead. After about five minutes the bleeding slows, but my head pounds like a mallet on a bass drum.

With my good eye, I see Sgt. Moses enter the latrine. I lean against the cement wall while Pit wipes at the floor and sink.

"Are you okay, Dowdell?" Moses leans over me again.

"I'm okay, Sarge."

He pulls the towel away to see for himself.

"You need to see a medic, Dowdell. Turner, you go with him. Inform them that I sent you, and tell them there was an accident during the excavation work in the southeast quadrant. Tell them Private Dowdell tripped over a shovel, and hit his head on a rock."

Before we can catch ourselves, Pit and I share a glance of disbelief.

"Yes sir, Sarge," Pit recovers first, but Moses has seen the look between us.

"Look boys, you've heard about the trouble that's going on at Fort Lawton. They damn near had a race riot. An Italian prisoner of war was killed, and all the Negro soldiers involved went to jail. We can't have that here."

"Sarge, you know them white boys started the fight, right? They followed us, and insulted us." Pit was angry.

"I know, Turner. But I'm telling you what to say at the hospital, and don't you start running off at the mouth when you get there."

Moses' warning is accompanied by one of the angry stares he saves just for Pit. The two glare at each other for a moment, then the Sarge turns on his heels, and marches out of the latrine all spit and polish again.

Pit helps me up from the floor, and I look in the mirror. My left eye is swollen shut, a gash on my head is still bleeding, and I also have a fat lip.

"Damn, I sure do look a mess."

"Don't worry," Pit jokes, "you was never that good looking anyway."

"What was the Sergeant saying about Fort Lawton?" I manage to slur.

"Didn't you hear? There was a fight between white and colored soldiers, and a prisoner was found hung the next day. Now, why in the world would we be lynching somebody? Everybody knows who does the lynching in the U.S. of A."

Pit pound his fist into the palm of his hand. I'd never seen him so angry. "LeRoy, I'm not gonna take no shit from these white boys. If another one of them confronts me, it's gonna be hell to pay. And, Moses better get off my back, too. I don't think I can take much more of this, man."

"I hear you, Pit," is all I can think to say. Then my knees give away.

Chapter 15

(Pit/Georgette)

It is nearly a quarter mile to the base hospital, and I half
walk and half drag LeRoy to get him there, then push him
through the door and guide him to the nearest bench. I'm
sweating like a hog, and have to catch my breath so I slump into
the seat next to him. LeRoy has another wet towel to his head,
and it is pink instead of red which is a good sign.

A white woman in civilian clothes at the front desk gives us
the eye, and I wave her off because I need more time before I
can answer her questions. She responds by getting up and
leaving through the door behind the desk. Moments later a
Negro nurse comes to the desk, picks up a small, brown clip
board and walks over to us.

"What happened to him?" She asks. I look over at LeRoy
who stares at me with his good eye, and tries to straighten
himself on the bench.

"There was an accident at the construction field," I lie.

"Oh yeah, we heard about that *accident*. A white soldier
was admitted to the main hospital an hour ago with a broken
arm, and another with a concussion. Then a half hour ago, one
of your buddies came in here asking to see the dentist to fix a
couple of loose teeth. That was some accident," the nurse says
making notes on the clipboard.

"What's your name soldier?" She aims her question at LeRoy.

"Dowdell, LeRoy. Private First Class," he says through puffy lips.

The nurse looks at LeRoy again, when she hears his name. "You the horn player?" she asks.

"Uh-huh."

"Well, I guess we better start working on that face, so you can play again. Right now, I don't think you could play a tuba," she says with a twinkle in her eye.

The name tag on her uniform reads: Goodwin, N.

LeRoy tries to respond to her friendly words, but the pain is really starting to get to him, so I decide to cut into his action with this pretty nurse.

"Well, I see you know a little something about our boy, here."

"Yes, I know who he is," Nurse Goodwin says with a cold look, and a surly tone. "I know about you, too."

She walks us down the hall to a small room with a cot and a couple of chairs. She tells LeRoy to sit on the bed. Although he isn't bleeding anymore, Goodwin presses a cold compress to his head and holds it there. She ignores me. Finally, a white doctor and another nurse come in to check on LeRoy. The doc orders a set of x-rays, and I go outside to wait. I need a cigarette and some fresh air.

130

I sit in the courtyard across from the hospital, and I'm on my second Lucky Strike when I see Georgette drive a Jeep up to the front door of the hospital, and rush through the main door. She has friends in every part of the camp. Someone must have called her about LeRoy, probably that ice cold nurse. When I finish my smoke, I return to the waiting area.

The white volunteer has returned to the front desk, and she gives me the look again. The waiting room is empty, so I find a nice corner chair, lean back against the wall, and close my eyes. This is a waste of time, but it beats working in the Arizona sun.

When I park my Jeep in the hospital lane, I see Pit across the yard having a smoke. I don't hail him, and I don't think he even sees me, which is a good thing because I don't have time for pleasantries this afternoon. I have to see how LeRoy is doing. News of the fight is all over the base. The story is Sgt. Moses used his baton to break it up, and if he hadn't come along when he did, things might have been much worse. Sylvester lost a tooth in the fight, and LeRoy was kicked unconscious, but folks are saying our guys got the best of them white boys. *Good.* Mama would be angry with me for that thought. "It ain't ever Christian to wish somebody harm, Sis," she would say. But today I am thinking that sometimes you have to apply a little eye for an eye.

Nadine shows me LeRoy's chart as soon as I arrive in the nurses' area; she had called fifteen minutes ago to tell me of LeRoy's head injury. There is really no breach of regulations because I will get his medical record to file in a couple of weeks anyway. If I wanted, I could get information about practically anyone on the base. Only a few, highly-confidential records are not in the files that I collect and organize every day. According to the patient form, LeRoy has no fracture. Nadine tells me the white doctor has seen the x-ray, and turned the case over to the Negro head nurse with the appraisal: "he's one hard-headed boy, Frankie, you can take it from here." Corporal Frankie Mae Lee had cleaned LeRoy's open wound and put in a few stitches above his cheekbone and he will be staying overnight for observation.

"There's only one other guy in the infirmary, Georgette, who had his tonsils removed yesterday. So, why don't you go ahead and look in on LeRoy."

"Thanks, Nadine. Is it true one of the white soldiers has a broken arm?"

"Yes, and it's a bad break, but he's being treated in the other wing."

I scan the infirmary for LeRoy, and see him in a bed against the far wall. The soldier recovering from the tonsillectomy lifts himself up on his elbow, and tries to give me a wolf whistle as I pass his bed. I smile at him and give him a thumb's up. As I get closer to LeRoy's cot, I can see the damage of the kicks. The left side of his face is very swollen and deep purple spreads from the edges of the wound near his eye. He has a bandage at his scalp line where Frankie has sewn in the few stitches he needed. If we were alone, I would kiss his good cheek. But the soldier with the healing throat is looking at us with great interest. LeRoy senses someone is near and turns his head in my direction.

"Hi sugar," he speaks with the slowness of waking, and pain medication. "It's good to see you."

"That's private, soldier".

Fraternizing during duty is a serious offense, and I'm not even supposed to be in the infirmary. I can't stay long, but I need to see LeRoy for myself to make sure he's okay.

"Okay, Private Newton. Thanks for coming to see me."

"How are you feeling?" I ask keeping my voice low.

"How does it look like I'm feeling?"

"I have to admit not so good." I touch his hand that grips the brown, wool blanket. I've already forgotten my own warning about fraternizing, but LeRoy looks like a sick little boy and my heart aches for him. In this moment, I realize how important he has become to me. He closes his good eye and starts talking.

"Georgie, I didn't come here to be treated like the enemy. I thought the idea was to hate the Japs and Krauts, but the army hates us even more. They say this war is about fighting for

133

freedom, but they don't care about none of that. When they look at us they just see niggers in the white man's uniform."

"Don't use their word, LeRoy," I say gently. "We're Negroes, and American soldiers. They can't make us anything less, unless we let them."

I recall the anger I felt just a half hour ago. I understand LeRoy's feelings but I don't want him to get worked up, he needs to rest. There is nothing he can do about prejudice from this hospital room except to get strong again. Sgt. Moses was overheard saying that LeRoy, Pit, Sylvester and Bennie had been baited by the white soldiers, and they stood up for each other. "There is no greater honor than to stand up for your friend," he had said. Apparently Moses also admitted he might have been wrong about Pit.

"You and the guys could have gotten into real trouble, LeRoy, even court-martialed."

"I know, but we aren't gonna let those crackers tell us the only thing we're good for is digging holes."

He winces in pain and pulls up against his pillows.

"Georgie have you heard anything about us getting to go to the fight?"

He won't like what I've heard, or seen. I've been preparing deployment papers for hundreds of soldiers over the last week. More than a thousand soldiers are being sent to Europe next week, and another 3,000 next month. But, deployment numbers for the all-Negro 92nd infantry division are much, much lower.

"Don't worry about that now. You just get some rest, soldier."

I lean over him and give him a tender touch on his good cheek. The soldier a few cots away manages a whistle.

"Okay, Private sugar," he whispers.

Chapter 16

(Sgt. Moses)

Following the attack on Pearl Harbor, Ft. Huachuca grew to almost 50,000 people at the base and among them, several thousand civilian workers. But as the war progresses, the base numbers have dwindled to less than fifteen thousand. In two years, the other Negro non-coms and I have trained nearly five thousand colored soldiers on our side of the base, and the officers from the WAACS 32nd and 33rd auxiliary units have also trained hundreds of Negro female enlistees. Yet, only a few hundred of our recruits are being prepared for action overseas and most of that is for non-combat duty.

The women don't mind so much, but our men are reminded daily that their wartime service is not discernably more than was expected of them before the war. The feats of courage by the Tuskegee airmen, the Navy cook, Dorie Miller, who shot down six Japanese aircraft during the Pearl Harbor attack, and a quartermasters unit making a name for itself in North Africa, are reported by the mainstream press as oddities.

"Captain Hurley will see you now, Sgt. Moses."

I look at the colored corporal standing near the captain's door, he's one of the lucky ones with a job that doesn't involve hard labor. I rise from the chair, making sure my shirt is still tucked in, and secure my cap under my arm.

"Go right in, sergeant," the Corporal says stepping aside and holding the door.

Captain Hurley is focused on a document atop his desk. He doesn't look up, but I present a salute as regulations require. Finally, he locks his eyes on mine and takes his own, sweet time returning the salute. I drop my hand and stand at attention.

"What's this I hear about a fight with some of the boys in your unit, Moses?"

I realized an hour after the fight, that I couldn't keep a lid on this thing...everyone was talking about it, but I thought we might be able to keep it among us soldiers. But, Hurley knows.

"I don't know what you heard, captain," my voice is low and even, the way I always speak to the brass. "It was a soldiers' scuffle, that's all there was to it."

"A scuffle, you say," Hurley repeats the word, then lifts a paper from the file in front of him. "One broken arm, a concussion, one dental procedure and a man still in the hospital for observation. That's one hell of a scuffle, sergeant," he snarls. "Now, don't get me wrong, I know your boys are going to show high spirits every now and then. That's their nature. But when a white soldier gets his arm broken in a brawl with your roughneck Nigras, that's going too far."

I can't stop a wince, but quickly restore my poker face. Hurley believes he knows the nature of Negroes because he was raised around us, and his father employs a hundred colored workers at their farm in Alabama. He thinks it's his calling to tell the Negro officers what he thinks of our troops, and how they ought to be managed. Often he gives these opinions in front of white officers and non-coms. I clear my throat.

"Captain, my troops tell me the white soldiers started this altercation." I use the ten-dollar word on purpose, because I know it drives him crazy when we display any sign of education or culture.

Hurley stares at me with venom in his eyes for what must be thirty seconds, his body rigid, his hands knotted on his desk. "Stand at ease, Sergeant Moses," he finally says leaning back in his chair and lacing his hands behind his neck. His mood changes so quickly it takes me by surprise.

"Moses, you have a good track record in your three years here at Huachuca." Hurley leans over the folder on his desk. So, it's *my* file, he is reading.

"Yes, sir, thank you, sir."

I stand at ease but my guard isn't down. Hurley opens the folder again and runs his finger down one of the pages.

"I see here, that you've trained over eight hundred recruits. You keep them on the straight and narrow, and you don't put up with any crybabies."

"No sir."

"So, you're from Chicago? That's a big city."

"Yes sir."

"I've never been to Chicago. I hear they have a lot of gangs there, and even more liberals."

I think maybe Hurley is trying to bait me, so I just keep quiet, and shift my weight from one leg to the other. He keeps staring at me so I speak up. "Chicago is doing a heck of a job supporting the war effort, sir. They're building lots of armaments and parts for bomber planes."

Hurley considers that information and gives me a nod.

"You know there was a race riot at a base on the west coast with nearly seventy-five soldiers involved. The newspapers have been asking lots of questions, so the War Department is issuing new policies for the way we, uh, do things."

"Yes sir." I wonder where all this is leading.

"We're going to try a couple of new procedures at Huachuca, Moses. We're going to put together an integrated music corps for parades, ceremonies and the like."

"What?" I ask, before I can stop the question.

"What's that, Sergeant?"

"Sir, you mean there won't be two separate bands anymore?"

"There will still be two base bands, Moses. But there will be a third group. A mixed group of musicians, the best we have, and a new, mixed color guard."

"I see, captain."

"No, I don't think you *do* see, sergeant." Hurley leans back in his chair again. "You, and Sergeant Terry will be in charge of this new corps. The unit will practice together as a band, work together on general duties and eat together at a new mess hall we're opening."

I am stunned. Not only do I not like Sgt. Terry—he and I have exchanged heated words on numerous occasions—but the whole concept is absurd. It won't work. The Negro soldiers may go along with it, but the white soldiers will rebel.

"Nothing to say, sergeant?"

"No sir," my mouth is dry and the words come out sluggishly.

"It's a grand experiment, good for the army and good for Huachuca," Hurley recites in a monotone, practicing what he will be telling all the skeptics.

"Why have I been selected for this duty?" I manage to say when the spit finds its way back into my mouth.

"You come highly recommended by the other non-coms and even some of the officers, Moses. You have a reputation for being *regular* Army," the Captain says with just a hint of disdain.

Then he is done. He dismisses me. I salute, and he reciprocates.

In the captain's anteroom, the corporal looks up from his desk. I was wrong, this soldier is doing very hard labor in supporting Captain Hurley.

"Good luck, sergeant", the corporal says sincerely.

He obviously knows all about this so-called experiment, and I'm sure I still look shell shocked.

"Thanks," I say, putting on my cap. "I'll need it."

Part Three

April 1944

Chapter 17

(LeRoy)

The order came down just yesterday. I am going overseas. The 'Ft. Huachuca All-American Freedom Marching Band' will make a tour of Europe in three months, but we are shipping out in six weeks because we are to perform in Washington, DC and New York City before we sail on the Dorothea Dix from New York, to Ireland.

The Freedom Band is a special, mixed-race, squad in a new, two-room barracks near the parade grounds. The white soldiers sleep and shower on one side of the building, and we have the other side. But we are together for work assignments, band practice, and our meals. The camp is up in arms about the new unit. Some think it is a good idea, 'historic' they call it, and will show that the army is dealing with the conflicts between Negro and white soldiers. Others think the Freedom Band is just a sham. Pit says it doesn't matter one way or the other.

"Think about it, LeRoy. I don't care how they try to mix things up, it ain't gonna change the way coloreds and whites feel about each other."

"I'm not so sure Pit, some of the white guys are cool, you know. They just want to play music, and they don't care so much about color."

"When push comes to shove, you'll see how fast they stick together. That's the gospel, according to the way it is."

Maybe Pit is right, but for me, the Freedom Band is a way to fulfill my dreams. I'm eager to visit the cities where great composers lived hundreds of years before. Although jazz and the music of the church, have filled my past time, it's Bach, Mozart, Beethoven and even John Philip Sousa that makes me imagine places I've never been.

Georgie shares my curiosity about the world. A few times, she and I have sneaked away from our group to see a picture show. From the balcony, we've watched the newsreels showing grand places where rich people step out on the town wearing beautiful clothes, furs, jewelry and top hats, and we dream about how it would feel to be among these fine people. The guys and girls in our crowd and even our families would laugh at these ideas, but I know Georgie understands my excitement about visiting some of the places we've seen at the movies.

The Freedom Band director, Lieutenant Saul Bergen, is impressed with my playing. He hasn't told me himself, but Jessup, one of the white horn players, let it slip one day during a break in band practice. I was playing around with some licks I heard on a Doc Cheatham record.

"Well, I'll be damned, boy," Jessup pulled up a chair to listen. "Like Bergen said, you do play like you taken over by the black devil himself."

"Why the devil got to be black, Jessup?" I asked, ignoring the compliment.

"That's the way Bergen said it, that's all. I didn't mean any offense."

"Well, well alright then," I said.

Jessup was embarrassed, and didn't look at me again as he rose to rejoin the white band members. My reaction even took me by surprise. Maybe I've let Pit's words sink into me, and I expect an insult from the white guys, even when there isn't one intended. Maybe that kind of reaction, is the reason the Freedom Band isn't going all that well.

Moses and Terry try hard to pretend they get along with each other, but it's clear to all of us it's just for show. We eat together, march together and spend long hours of practice together, but there's too much history between us to change our ways overnight. And it's not just the white soldiers, many of our guys make fun of the way the white boys eat, or talk, and we always joke about how much better we are at marching. Even Bergen admits our superiority on the parade field, and has worked out a formation that puts a Negro soldier next to a white soldier, so the band will look the part and keep better time.

We have a performance scheduled for the VIPs before we leave base, so Hurley comes by often to hear and see us practice, and he is not shy about criticizing Sgt. Moses.

"Your boys don't seem to have the right attitude about this assignment, Moses," Hurley has said in front of the full band. "This is work. You're not here to have fun. Look at Sgt. Terry's men, they're getting better and better with the marching patterns because they take this work seriously."

Moses just keeps his cool when Hurley criticizes us, but one of the bartenders at the non-coms club told me the Sarge comes in almost every night to get drunk and curse under his breath about Hurley and Terry. The bartender says Moses calls them the cracker brothers.

My plan is to get through all of this race stuff by doing what I'm told, playing music, and keeping my head down. Once the Freedom Band begins touring, things will settle into a pattern, and once I get out of the army and join a real band, I don't think my skin color will matter as much as how I play my horn. Then, maybe Georgie and I can get married and move to New York City, or maybe Chicago, and we can live the life we've both dreamed about. *But, I haven't even asked her to wait for me and maybe she'll only wait if we're engaged.* A lump forms in my throat, as I think this.

All this daydreaming about the band and Georgie are distracting me from the new composition I'm working on. I've

145

found a corner table in the recreation hall and I'm trying to concentrate on my arrangement, when I hear Pit approaching.

"Hey man, whatcha doing?"

Pit throws himself into the chair across from me—he doesn't do anything in a small way. He snatches my sheet music from the table, and looks at it.

"What's this man, jazz or some of that snooty music you like?" his eyes squint as he tries to make sense of my notations.

"It's a jazz piece I'm working on. So what's going on with you? I thought you were spending the rest of the day with Loretta? You two looked pretty cozy when you left church."

"Aw, man, Loretta is starting to get on my nerves. She's mad because I went out with that Mexican girl, Anna. I told her I'm just having a little fun, but Loretta's trying to act like she owns me, and she don't."

"You mean Private Alvarado in the quartermaster's office?"

"Yep. Little Anna," Pit chuckles. "She's got that long hair and them big legs. She barely comes up to my shoulder, but she's all woman, you know what I mean, Leroy?" Pit grins.

"I did hear that she likes colored guys."

It is a simple statement, because I don't want to open the door for Pit's further views on women. When he sees I don't have any more to say about Anna, he offers an invitation.

"Hey, you want to go over to the tavern with me and Sylvester and have a few beers?"

"No, I can't this time. I need to finish up this music, and then I'm gonna meet a couple of the guys in the band to hear what it sounds like. You want to come over and listen?"

"Man, I don't want to sit around and watch you fools fiddle around. I work hard all week, and I only have one day free, so I want to blow off some steam. You're changing LeRoy, you know that? I hope you're not forgetting your old friends."

I can tell Pit is serious. I think he and some of the other guys are jealous that my work in the band will get me where they all want to be: overseas and closer to the action. The truth is, the band won't travel anywhere near the frontlines but still there are hard feelings.

"Pit, I ain't changing, but I got a letter that my music teacher, you've heard me talk about him, is coming here to see me. I want to be sure I have this piece finished so I can give it to him."

Pit flings the sheet music onto the table and his chair scrapes loudly against the floor when he stands, attracting the curious glances of those nearby.

"Well, do what you gotta do, LeRoy," he says and leaves without another word.

It takes a few minutes to regain my focus. Despite what Pit thinks, I really do miss the guys in my old unit. We've stuck together through thick and thin, and I feel like I have real friends for the first time in my life. But we do spend less time together now, and maybe we are drifting apart.

Mr. Giles has also become a friend and I'm excited about his visit. I know he doesn't have a lot of money, and doesn't leave his mother all that often, but somehow he has arranged for two weeks off to see a friend in Mexico, and his train will bring him through Tucson. I have a lot to tell him: about the band, the upcoming trip to Europe, and about Georgie. Another lump gathers and I can't swallow, so I try clearing my throat. It doesn't help. I'm feeling uncertain, like that night on the train before we arrived at Huachuca. And there's something else, a familiar stirring, but I can't put my finger on it. Maybe it's just nerves.

Chapter 18

(Georgette)

After yearning for distance from Pender, I can't explain why I still think of home every day, and call several times a month for news of family and friends. Lately the news I crave is of Boone, whose letters have become more and more infrequent. I've grown close to LeRoy, but I have a bond with Boone that has not been broken—at least not on my part. Whenever I ask mama about Boone she responds by saying she either did or did not see him in church the previous Sunday. When I ask about him today, I'm surprised by her response.

"Sis, Boone has been drafted."

"Drafted?"

"He's going to be with the Tuskegee Airman. We're all so proud of him."

Mama tells me what she's heard from Mrs. Mack, that Boone's skills as a mechanic, trumped the farm role that had given her son a waiver from military service up to now. I know something mama doesn't. Boone has desperately wanted to enlist, but his father has begged him to stay home. Now that he is drafted, I'm sure it is a tense time in his home.

I hold my breath as the phone rings at the Mack farm. Each soldier is allotted fifteen minutes of phone time every ten days, and I have always used these precious minutes to call mama, but today I need to hear Boone's voice. It's just before supper time so he should be home, maybe sitting on the front porch with his father discussing next week's work, or enjoying a game of horseshoes, maybe even tinkering with an engine or some other piece of equipment. When Boone's mother picks up the phone, my heart is racing.

"Hi, Mrs. Mack," I sound like a school girl.

"Who's this?" Mrs. Mack asks with curiosity.

"This is Georgette Newton. I'm calling from Arizona."

"Well, Georgette, it's been a long time since I heard your voice. How are you doing, baby? Your mama tells me you're getting along real fine with those Army gals."

"Yes, ma'am. I'm doing fine, and you?"

"Oh, we're all doing well. But, we sure do miss seeing you. Boone showed us that picture you sent, wearing your uniform, and you look real good in it, Georgette. You know Boone is going to be leaving for the Army himself next month."

Now my heart sinks. I didn't know he'd be leaving so soon. Why hadn't he told me?

"Yes, ma'am, mama told me about that."

"Georgette, I'm gonna miss my boy. I know he's a man now, but I been washing and cooking and mending for him for

22 years and in a little while he'll be all the way in another country. Things are moving so fast, why he..."

"Yes, ma'am, I know," I try a gentle interruption. "Is Boone home? Can I talk to him?"

"Oh I'm sorry, Georgette I am just going on and on. No, Boone isn't here. He's having dinner with the Briscoe's."

My heart sinks again. LuAnn Briscoe is my chief rival for Boone's affections. I know Boone thinks LuAnn is pretty, and she has set her cap for him.

"Are you there, Georgette?" Mrs. Mack asks in a loud voice shaking me from my miserable thoughts.

"Yes ma'am, I'm here. Will you please tell Boone that I called and that I'll call him again on Wednesday, after your supper?"

"I sure will do that, Georgette. You take good care of yourself now."

When I hang up I notice the line for phones is so long it winds around one corner of the hall. Phone etiquette is a serious thing at Ft. Huachuca. With thousands of enlisted men and women wanting to speak to loved ones, everyone keeps their calls short. I've seen near fist fights between soldiers over the five-minute call rule. It's one of the informal rules of the base, like not asking for more than two scoops of potatoes in the mess, or not fraternizing too much with those outside your race.

The no fraternizing rule doesn't hold true for mixing with the Mexicans in town, or on base. In Arizona, there are a lot of Mexican soldiers and a few dozen Mexican WAACS. I have seen the Negro enlisted men chase after these girls with their light brown skin and good hair. Pit is talking to one of them now outside the door of the recreation hall. I wave to him, and he waves back. LeRoy isn't with him and I'm glad, because I want to be alone to do some thinking.

Chapter 19

(Pit)

I ran into Anna as I was leaving the recreation hall. She has a two-day leave and is on her way into town. She wears a white skirt that shows off her legs, and has on that red lipstick I like. She wants to know when we're going out again, so I sweet talk her for a while. I notice Georgette hurrying out the east door and hope she won't mention to Loretta that she's seen me with Anna. Damn, that's all I need. As big as this base is, it can be tricky keeping your love life to yourself. Anna and I go our separate ways and I head to the tavern. It seems everybody has something to do this afternoon, so I'll get a drink and maybe play a game of ping pong.

The tavern is busy. Soldiers are playing cards in groups of three or four at every table, a few guys shoot craps in the far corner near the juke box, both pool tables are in use, and a ping pong game is underway. Sylvester and Bennie are in one of the card games so I sit at the bar, order a beer and have a chat with Al, the bartender. Al is an older guy, a civilian, but he likes sports and we talk all the time about baseball.

"Things are really hopping today, Al."

"It's been busy all afternoon. One of the Negro companies is being deployed tomorrow, and people are celebrating."

"Yeah, I heard. Too bad it's not me," I say taking a long pull of my beer.

The excitement I had about the army is pretty much gone. When I got drafted, it was a relief, because I didn't really have any other place to go. But now I'm feeling itchy to get into the action. Any kind of action.

"How is your unit making out, Pit. You guys still working on the new recreation building?"

"I tell you one thing, Al. I thought army life was going to be different. I am sick of digging holes, and I'm sick of unloading supplies."

"You're from Georgia ain't you, man?" Al asks.

"Yup, from Bluffton."

"You still got people there?"

"Not to speak of."

I changed the subject to Jackie Robinson. I've only told LeRoy a little bit about my thirteen years at the orphanage which was my home before the army. At Brickstone, I'd been a leader. The boys and girls looked up to me, and as I got older Miss Marsh counted on me to watch out for the younger kids. I was good at it. I didn't have much use for school, but I made sure the boys got up on time, got washed up and had their breakfast, so they could catch the school bus on weekdays. Miss Marsh often repeated the story of how I didn't say a word to anyone when I first came to Brickstone at five years old. I wouldn't let anybody touch me. Whenever I went missing, she would find me in the orchard, sitting at the trunk of one of the peach trees, eating any fruit that had fallen or been dropped by the birds. She was the one who gave me the nickname 'Pit', and anytime she wanted me to do something she'd bribe me with a peach. That's how she got me to take baths.

"Jerome, I got this big, ripe, juicy peach for you", she'd say and when I reached for it she'd pull it away. "You can have it, but first you got to find it," then she'd drop the peach into a tub of soapy water. I'd climb into the tub, clothes and all, searching the bottom until I found the peach, and eat it right then and there with suds up to my neck.

At thirteen, I was hiring out with the local farms and no one asked why I wasn't in school. By the time I was sixteen, I was grooming horses, curing hams and supervising the picking crews that came to town each summer. I gave Miss Marsh some of the money I earned-though she never asked for it-and I kept the rest for courting a few of the girls in town, and buying the things I needed to play baseball in the county league. I was a big man in Bluffton. Most of the folks thought I just worked at the orphanage, they didn't know I was a resident. When I left, I told folks I was going to the army to be a war hero, and nobody doubted that I would do just that.

Memories of my mother always came in bits and pieces fading in and out before I could really name them. Soft hands, a touch of cotton against my cheek, bouncing on a thick lap, the fragrance of rose water, the stinging odor of urine, loud angry voices, the shadowy figures of different men who took her away from my outstretched arms, unanswered cries for milk, for attention, for love. Sometimes at the orphanage I'd stretch face down on the meadow grass to get closer to these recollections of a mother I never really knew.

Sylvester loses his card game and joins me to lean against the bar. "Did you talk to LeRoy, is he coming over?"

"No, he's meeting some of his new friends. He's put us down, Syl. Now that he's with that damn Freedom Band."

"I wish I was in the band so I could get my ass off this base," Sylvester said.

"Yeah, well if I was getting ready to ship off, I'd remember who my real friends are."

"Aw Pit, you know how it is. We're all here just doing our time. We might not ever get to see any real action, so we're just making the best of it. Collecting our pay, doing what they tell us to do and waiting to see what's in store for us on the other side of the war. I wouldn't mind being in the fight, but at least here we ain't dying. You know what I mean?"

I see Loretta and Clarice come into the tavern. I give them a wave, and Clarice waves back, but Loretta ignores me.

"You still in the shit house with Loretta, I see." Sylvester says.

"Yeah, I guess I am.

"What about Clarice. She's a good egg, you ever think about getting next to her, Pit?"

"Nah, she ain't my type, and neither is Georgette."

"Now I wouldn't mind having me some of that Georgette. She's a pretty thing, but LeRoy seems to have her wrapped up tight."

"Don't be fooled, Syl. LeRoy don't know how to handle women. She probably do need a real man."

"I bet she wouldn't give either one of us the time of day. Georgette seems like one of them church-going girls who wants to have fun, but not the wrong kind of fun."

I know exactly what Sylvester means about Georgette. That's why I prefer Loretta, she appreciates having a good time with a man.

"I'm gonna work my game better with Loretta," I announce.

"You still seeing that Anna girl?"

"Yeah, but I know how to juggle a couple of women. Damn I've juggled more women than that. I don't know why I'm letting Loretta get under my skin. Women are always jealous, it comes with the territory."

Lately, I'd been thinking I might be the one who's jealous— of LeRoy. But that's not something I would ever tell anyone. He and I used to be real tight, but now we hardly see each other. He's getting a lot of attention playing with that band, the kind of attention I used to get when I played baseball. I'm a better man than LeRoy in every way, but on this damned base I don't have any opportunity to shine.

"I hear Sgt. Moses is taking a leave before he ships off base with the Freedom Band," Sylvester cuts into my thoughts. "The way I hear it, he hasn't taking time off since the war started, and now he's going to be gone ten days."

"Good riddance, if you ask me. You know, I could have looked up to him if he wasn't such a son of a bitch."

"Yeah, he can be tough alright but he has a reputation for being a hell of a soldier. Anyway, LeRoy gets to deal with Moses now." Sylvester says finishing off his beer.

"Good riddance to both of them, man. Come on let's go talk to the girls."

Sylvester and I stroll over to Loretta and Clarice.

"Can we buy you ladies a beverage?" I say using my tried-and-true approach.

"We're having a private conversation," Loretta says icily.

"Well, we're privates," I respond to get a laugh.

"First-class, privates," Sylvester adds trying to build on my game.

Loretta rolls her eyes, but Clarice is softening up and chuckles at our lame humor. I pull a chair over from another table and flop in it. Sylvester sits too.

"So, what are you girls talking about?" I ask.

"No-account men," Loretta says immediately.

I try to break the freeze. "I saw Georgette over at the rec hall, but she seemed in a hurry."

"She's got a lot on her mind," Clarice says taking a sip from her Coke.

"You mean she's got LeRoy on her mind," Sylvester says.

"There's more to think about than just men," Loretta says still pouting. "Some of us girls would like to get overseas, too, you know. There are non-combat jobs we can do."

"I wish I could get in the fight," I say signaling for more drinks.

"Well, at least LeRoy will have a chance to see what it looks like away from Huachuca," Loretta says.

Sylvester and Clarice murmur their agreement.

I want to be happy for LeRoy but I can't. He isn't half the man or soldier I am. I order a scotch and hold my tongue.

Chapter 20
(Boone)

Things are happening fast. Not three weeks ago, my only concern was whether we should put in some corn in our east acres instead of tobacco. Both are cash crops in the war economy, but corn has more consumer uses. Now, in a month I'll be a member of the Tuskegee Airmen and a world away from this farm.

I'll have the chance to work on airplanes. The Tuskegee Airmen are flying P-40 Warhawks into Europe and North Africa and some of my friends have already warned me of the danger I'll face. I'm not afraid of the combat duty and I'm not worried that our farm will fail without me. Only one thing weighs heavy on my heart, and that is the thought of losing Lil.

When mama told me of her phone call, I sorted things out real fast. LuAnn has made it clear that if I want to make our relationship formal before I leave, she'll make a home for us until I return. She's a pretty girl with long wavy hair and hazel eyes, and when we've parked the truck up at Flood's Peak, LuAnn has let me go a lot farther than Lil ever did. But it's Lil that I love. She told mama she'd call again on Wednesday but I can't wait that long to let her know how things are, so I'm writing her a letter. It's not like any of the letters I've sent before, and she won't even receive it before she phones, but I want to get my feelings out on paper.

There are only a few things about a woman that makes a man want to give up his single life. The promise of good relations is one of them, and a sense that she is the person you want to raise your children. But the most important thing for me, is that Lil and I can really talk to each other. I have shared my deepest thoughts with her and I know she is the one I will be content to listen to for the rest of my life. That's what I write in the letter.

I put the single page into an envelope, lick the flap and seal it firmly, then walk the mile and a half into town to post the letter. When Lil calls in three days, I will ask her to wait for me and for marriage. I know she has been changed by her time in the Army, but I hope she still feels for me what I do for her. I also hope she's experienced enough adventure over the last six months, to want to return to Pender to make a life with me.

Chapter 21

(Georgette)

LeRoy will soon travel to New York City, and then throughout Europe, to places he and I have talked about visiting together. My dreams of hurrying through crowded streets dressed in stylish clothes and tardy for some grand appointment have become less frequent. It's not that I don't still want to see New York City, Chicago or St. Louis, but I've come to know that people out in the world, aren't that much smarter or interesting, and certainly not better, than those I've left behind.

The Army has also taught me a lot more about white folks than I ever knew. In the rural south, poor white and colored people mingle everyday just doing average things. The railroad tracks separate their side of town from ours, but that divide mostly affects where we live, not how we actually spend our days. In Pender, whites own most of the stores we shop in, but when we take our crops to the market we stand side by side with them. There are two churches and separate schools, but the post office and town hall is for everybody. If you need to pay taxes, register your truck, or see the sheriff about missing chickens, whites and coloreds enter the same heavy door, and wait in the same long line.

The army is different. Here, white people control every aspect of your life, and Jim Crow laws can't hold a candle to the sunup-to-sundown prejudice, and outright hatred, we face in the military. You can see it in their eyes—officers, enlisted men, even the civilians.

An incident with a recruit just a few weeks ago proved it to me, again. I'd processed the papers of this nineteen-year-old from Arkansas—an emergency pass to attend his mother's funeral. I drove over to his barracks and his sergeant pointed him out to me.

"Private Welch?"

He looked up at me from his packing. He was stuffing socks, and skivvies into his duffel. His shaving kit lay on his bunk along with a picture of an older woman who I guessed was his mother.

"Yes, I'm Welch," he said slowly. I think I startled him. It was very unusual to see a Negro, let alone a woman in the men's barracks.

"I'm PFC Newton, and I have your emergency pass, travel documents and bus vouchers."

He saw me looking at the picture on his bunk, and quickly stuffed it into his bag.

"I'm sorry to hear about your mother," I said.

He stared coldly at me and did not acknowledge my expression of sympathy. I pulled the papers from my courier bag.

"You have to sign for these, Private Welch." I handed him the receipt form and a pen.

He squinted as he looked at the form, and I could tell he was trying to make out the words.

"Where do I sign?" he asked gruffly.

"Right there," I pointed to the line just below the signature of the base captain.

The way Welch held the pen was awkward, and he began to write his name with great difficulty. I realized he probably didn't read or write very well.

"The letter says that you have an emergency furlough and that you're due back on base in ten days. The Army is advancing your pay for the time you're gone."

Welch jerked his head up to look at me. "Who do you think you are, you nigra cunt?"

His words were a slap. I took two steps back from his bunk, and his sergeant approached us.

"Is there a problem, Welch?"

"This nigra shouldn't be in our barracks," Welch said finishing his signature and handing the letter to the sergeant.

I stood silent. The sergeant quickly scanned the form and handed it to me. He held out his hand for Welch's documents and I obliged. I took another step back before I turned to leave. I was sitting in my Jeep and shaking when the sergeant came out the barracks door and walked over to the vehicle.

"He just lost his mama, Private Newton," the sergeant said by way of explanation.

I nodded to him with appreciation that he even wanted to explain, and he watched as I started the engine, put the truck in gear, and drove away.

I release the memory of Private Welch, replacing it with thoughts of Boone and LeRoy. I just don't know how to choose between them. Boone is steady and smart. He respects me and makes me feel like his equal. I've imagined being his wife many times but the idea could never dampen my restlessness and ambitions. Now that Boone is joining the Airmen, I wonder if I'll ever see him again.

LeRoy has been pressuring me to be more intimate in our relationship. It is a sudden change, considering our relationship so far has consisted of kissing and hand-holding. But there is a burning in LeRoy's eyes I haven't seen before. It frightens me...and excites me.

I carry thoughts of my two sweethearts to bed. When LeRoy kisses me, I am outside of myself. His skill as a horn player shows itself in a particular way when we kiss, and on a couple of occasions his very talented tongue explored my ear until I nearly swooned. Boone and I have necked and petted but even when his kisses are urgent, there is still gentleness. LeRoy is charming, sensitive and more boy than man; while Boone's masculinity is effortless. Boone and I can talk for hours, but I also have great conversations with LeRoy, and we can share long, comfortable silences. My feelings for LeRoy are connected to my desires to be someone different than people expect of me, yet Boone loves me for who I already am.

I can hear mama's voice: "Sis, you always see things one way or the other, your daddy is like that too. Truth is, it ain't ever that simple." I wonder if I can ever talk to mama about Boone and LeRoy. I'm pretty sure if I told her, she'd tell daddy. So, for now I'll just confide in Clarice and Loretta.

I lift my head from the pillow and look down the long row of bunks toward Loretta's cot. She isn't moving. It's still many hours before daylight and Loretta likes to get her beauty rest. I look over my shoulder toward Clarice in the next bunk and I'm surprised to see her head also raised.

"You alright?" she whispers.

"Yeah, I just can't sleep."

"Well, I *can*," she says and turns pulling her blanket over her shoulders.

I drift to sleep thinking about the summer storms at home. The cottony clouds collapse quickly, spreading gray in all directions, the air arcs with electricity and becomes momentarily still, then the sky opens and rain furiously pelts everything in its reach. The torrent subsides, and then gently stops. The clouds embrace again in softness, and the sun lifts the fresh smell of earth into the air.

The next day, I'm still making the comparisons between LeRoy and Boone. I've allowed Loretta and Clarice to read Boone's letter, but they aren't much help in clarifying my choices.

"Wow, he says he wants to marry you, Georgette?" Clarice tells me what I already know.

"I know, but if I marry him that means moving back home."

"Would you go back?" Clarice asks.

"To be honest, I'm not sure. All I've wanted for the past year is to get away from Pender."

"Is Boone as fine as LeRoy?" Loretta asks focusing on what's most important to her.

"LeRoy *is* good looking," Clarice nods her head for emphasis, "but I've heard you say Boone is a handsome guy, too."

"They're both handsome, in different ways," I say.

"Seriously, Georgette, you might break LeRoy's heart if you decide to marry your boy from home. Have you thought of that?"

It's Loretta's turn to make a good point.

"Wouldn't Boone be broken-hearted, too? He's known you a whole lot longer than LeRoy," Clarice says.

I didn't call Boone on Wednesday as I'd promised and now that I have his letter, I'm not sure I'll call at all. Boone is so certain we should be together but I'm not.

"What if Boone is just being sentimental because he's being drafted?" I ask my friends.

"Boone's letter seems sincere, but we all know soldiers who have girls back home, and all the while they're chasing every skirt they can find here on base," Clarice reminds us and we all murmur our agreement.

"I just can't stop thinking about LeRoy?"

"He is so fine," Loretta says again.

"All's fair in love and war," Clarice says.

"What?" Loretta asks.

"Girl, Shakespeare or somebody wrote that," Clarice says.

"What?" Loretta is still trying to follow the point.

Clarice and I look at each other and laugh.

"You know that English guy who wrote all the plays. Look, I'm not sure who said it," Clarice admits, "but it means whether you're fighting a war, or fighting for a man, it can be ugly business."

Loretta responds with defensiveness. "Well, I don't know about no Shakespeare, but I don't think that's even right. What's so fair about war?"

Taps sound over the camp loudspeakers. It is a sweet, slow, melancholy tune. It not only signals the end of the day, but reminds us of fallen soldiers and those still fighting. But tonight I'm not thinking about the sacrifices of war. The bugler's call makes me think of the way LeRoy uses his talented tongue, when he kisses me.

Chapter 22

(Mr. Giles)

Robert's letter convinces me to go to him before he ships
off. He is usually confident and proud of his work, but now he's
uncertain whether he is making a difference. I'm worried about
him. He offered to take the train to Georgia, but we'll have
more time together if I make the trip. The Lord works in
mysterious ways, and last Sunday when the pastor announced
that a Florida congregation would use our church for a ten-day
revival—bringing their choir and music director with them—I
knew it was my opportunity to see Robert.

On the way, I'll visit with LeRoy. By all accounts, he is
doing well, certainly better than if he'd remained in Americus.
He really isn't the soldier type, but it was a good idea for him to
leave this small-minded town and if the army provided his
escape, so be it.

When I learned LeRoy would be stationed at the same base
as Robert, I knew I'd be able to play a small role in his success
in the army. He reminds me so much of the young man I used to
be. I was also a talented musician, and my gift got the attention
of the adults in my church and school. The town gossips
whispered about me, and I was teased a lot at school, but music
opened many doors for me and I was lucky to have parents who
fully supported me. When I received a scholarship to attend the

conservatory, it was a world where I belonged. I rubbed elbows with the finest musicians in Chicago and some of them became my friends. I played in jazz clubs even before I could take a legal drink. After hours, I would sit in with the band members improvising a jazz song or playing concert music. This went on throughout my years in training, and following graduation I stayed in the city, working as a professional musician, and soaking up the habits and diverse allures of a sophisticated metropolis.

It was at the Green Door Lounge on the south side of Chicago that I met Robert. The depression was fresh in everyone's mind, but those with money still spent it on music, booze and the ladies. Robert came into the Green Door with two other soldiers, and three beautiful women dressed in the latest fashions. The band was doing an arrangement of *Body and Soul*, and I was playing piano and feeling good. It was one of those nights where my hands seemed to have their own will, and when that happens I just watch them work. When I'd finished my solo, there was an outburst of applause, and my hands let me take the credit.

Robert watched our set intently. His companions were laughing and drinking, but he was clearly focused on the music. When we finished he came over and put a twenty in the tip jar on my piano.

"I enjoyed your playing, man," his brown eyes locked onto mine.

"Thank you, man."

"I've seen you play before, at the conservatory."

"So, you like classical music, too?"

"I like all good music...and good musicians." He gave me a long look and added: "Play some Billy Strayhorn."

Robert and his group left after the first set, but not before I played *Lush Life* by Strayhorn. Several hours later, when I stepped through the rear of the Green Door to head home, he was waiting for me.

"I thought I'd buy you a drink. If you'll let me."

His tone made his intentions clear. Men like us have a way of recognizing each other.

"Well, I've been drinking all night. I usually go home and wind down with a cup of tea."

"Tea huh," Robert chuckled. He reached into the pocket of his coat and pulled out a small flask. "Can I add some of this, to sweeten it up?"

"I never argue about how a man takes his tea."

We walked the eight blocks to my apartment. It was three a.m. and Chicago's famous wind was noticeably absent—even the wind has to rest sometime. When we got to my door, Robert held my trumpet case as I sorted through my keys. I led the way up the stairs, and I could feel his eyes on me. I didn't even know this man and I was bringing him to my home. I made tea, and he made love to me. That was seven years ago, and Robert and I have been lovers ever since.

I haven't seen him in almost two years, the longest we've been apart, but since Pearl Harbor the war has been his priority. Now he says he needs me and I won't let him down.

Chapter 23
(LeRoy)

This morning, just before dawn, Sergeant Moses enters our barracks turning on lights, and pounding the foot of our bunks with his baton. It is his normal routine, but every day it is a rude surprise. We're expected to roll out of our beds immediately and head to the latrines to shower and shave. There are no exceptions unless a man is sick, and even then he is to announce his illness, get into uniform, and if he can walk, make his way to the hospital.

I have a day pass to meet Mr. Giles in Tucson, but I get up with the squad, take care of my morning hygiene, square away my sleeping area, and report for roll call. I'll have breakfast with the unit, and then return to the barracks while the rest of the guys begin four hours of parade drills, followed by band practice.

The bus to town departs at 0900 hours, so I have some time to kill. I clean one of my horns, and then make revisions to an arrangement for a trumpet and piano duet that I'm working on. Notation isn't one of my favorite things but in music class, Mr. Giles pounded it into our heads that playing is only half the work.

"A real musician," he would say, "should always be able to interpret music as written." He was a tough instructor, and taught music like it was arithmetic.

One of the soldiers cleaning the barracks shouts, 'Ten Hut'. I jump to my feet as Sgt. Moses re-enters the barracks and heads to my bunk.

"I understand you're going into town, Private Dowdell."

"Yes sergeant, I have a day pass, sir."

"You're not required to call me 'sir' Dowdell, you know regulations."

"Yes sir, Sergeant Moses," I say this so quickly I can't correct myself.

Moses looks at me with curiosity.

"You're handling yourself very well in the Freedom Band, Dowdell," he finally says.

"Thank you, suh…rgeant," I manage.

This is the first time the Sarge has given me a compliment when Sgt. Terry hasn't been around to overhear. He looks at me a few more seconds, then realizing he has nothing more to say, clears his throat. "Well, enjoy your visit today, Private," he says turning on his heels, and leaving the barracks at his usual quick pace.

I continue standing, puzzled why Sgt. Moses has stopped in to see me. Is he trying to be nice? Maybe he's feeling the pressure from all the attention our mixed company is getting. I

175

sit again on my bunk and recall Moses' final words. He wished me a good visit. How did he know I was meeting someone in town?

The bus arrives in Tucson right on time, and stops across the road from the train station. I look out front for Mr. Giles and when I don't see him, I go inside. His telegram says his train will come in from San Antonio, and a porter tells me the train is still a half hour from arriving. I sit at one of the long, stone benches in the station's colored section. I reach for my pack of Camels, tap it a couple of times to loosen a cigarette, then pull one free with my lips. I slip out the book of matches tucked in the cellophane package, strike a match, and light the tip in one easy motion. I take a long drag. The smoke stings my throat, but immediately calms my mind. I picked up the habit within a week of being at Huachuca. Cigarettes are cheap, easy to get and smoking gives me a way to fit in with the guys.

I lean against the wall and wait. The station is brightly lit. Polished wood floors, and blue and orange wall tiles reflect a half dozen twirling ceiling fans. The fans don't do much more than keep the hot air moving, but the stone bench and the tiles against my back feel cool. There are very few people in the station. Gas rationing means fewer passenger trains; and people travel by rail only if they have the means, or the need to get somewhere fast. Mr. Giles doesn't have a lot of money, so it must be important for him to see his friend in Mexico. I take another long drag on the Camel, and think how fortunate I am to be in the Freedom Band. I play music, hear music, and talk about music—it's what I love to do. After the initial excitement and pride of having a weapon, I know I'd much rather have my trumpet.

I've seen the photographs of our new parade uniforms. One is a standard army drab shirt and tie with the Freedom Band insignia, and special wool slacks with cuffs. The uniform for outdoor events is a heavier, green bomber-style jacket, with three brass buttons on each sleeve and a red, white and blue cravat for our necks. We will wear specially made dress hats with a small U.S. flag sewn into the crown, so that we will fly the colors for anyone watching from above. We've also been issued two pairs of patent leather dress shoes. We're becoming a unified group and in a month, we'll be performing in front of VIPs—musicians and soldiers, colored and white, shoulder to shoulder, playing *Stars and Stripes Forever*, *Battle Hymn of the Republic*, and *America the Beautiful*. Marching and playing proudly for one country.

A loudspeaker announces the arrival of Mr. Giles' train and I move to the gate. Dozens of passengers leave the train and after five minutes I begin to wonder if he's aboard, but then he steps down from the second car of the six-car train that will continue on to California. He carries a small suitcase and is

177

followed by a porter who handles a larger suitcase and a garment bag. His clothes are sharp as usual, and more than one person turns to take a second look at this well-dressed colored man.

He sees me, waves, and picks up his pace. When we are standing toe to toe he holds out his hand and I meet it with mine.

"You look fine, LeRoy," he says, smiling.

"You too, sir," I reply.

"I know I'm a bit late, and I'm eager to catch up with you for as long as we can. When do you have to be back to your base?" We walk toward the station entrance as we talk, followed by the porter.

"I have a pass which allows me to be off the base until nineteen hundred hours, uh, that's seven p.m. But, I have a date so I need to leave no later than four p.m."

"A date, you say. Well, you certainly make a dashing soldier in that uniform, LeRoy."

"Thank you, sir."

I'm embarrassed by the compliment, and I glance at the porter who busies himself with the bags. Mr. Giles has taken a room for the night at the colored boarding house in town and asks the porter to make sure his bags are sent there. Giles hands him a couple of folded dollar bills and the porter tips his cap leaving us in front of the station. Again, I wonder how he is able to afford this trip on his teacher's salary.

"So LeRoy, where should we go for lunch? Let's find someplace where we can just sit and talk for a while."

We walk over to Kenny's barbeque joint. It sure is a step up from Red's pool hall back home. There are several small, round tables up front with black and red chairs. The floor is covered with black and white speckled linoleum and across from the tables is an eight-seat, counter with a chrome bar along the back of the counter. In the rear of Kenny's are a jukebox, and picnic tables covered with red and white checkered tablecloths.

The cook and waitress at Kenny's show great interest in Mr. Giles, and so do the other diners. They are used to seeing soldiers, the regulars from the community, and sometimes the train porters who have overnight stays in Tucson. But they hardly ever see a colored man wearing a charcoal wool overcoat with a hat to match, a tailored, black pinstriped suit, and black and white spectator shoes, unless he is one of the musicians, actors or sports stars who come to town to entertain the colored troops. I can tell they are wondering who Mr. Giles might be.

We take seats at the bench tables near the jukebox, and then it occurs to me that maybe we should be eating at a fancier restaurant.

"Mr. Giles, is this place okay for you? We could go somewhere else."

"Oh this is just fine, Leroy. We'll be comfortable here, and it's a lot better than Red's, wouldn't you say?"

179

We both smile at that memory of Americus, and I'm reminded of the easy relationship I've always had with Mr. Giles. He and I seem to think alike. He is already taking off his topcoat and then his jacket, which he neatly folds on the bench next to him. He puts his hat on top of the pile of clothes and signals for me to sit across from him.

"Okay, so tell me everything you've been doing, and don't leave anything out."

Mr. Giles places his forearms on the table and leans towards me with anticipation.

"Well, I, I guess..." I stammer. "I pretty much told you everything in my letters."

"But LeRoy, you've only sent me three letters in the nine months you've been gone." His words rush out as if this has been weighing on his mind, and I feel he is blaming me for something.

"Well we don't have a lot of time for letter writing in the Army."

"LeRoy, I understand. It's just that I wanted to hear from you more often."

I'm wondering if Mr. Giles and I are that easy with each other after all. I pick up my menu, and the waitress is a welcome break from the uncomfortable pause in our conversation.

"What'll it be sirs?" she asks casually and take this close-up opportunity to give Mr. Giles a good once over.

"Why don't you order something good for us, LeRoy," Mr. Giles says to me.

"We'll have a couple of pulled-pork platters with coleslaw and corn-on-the cob. That comes with corn bread," I say to Mr. Giles. He gives me a nod.

"To drink?" the waitress asks in shorthand.

With just a moment of hesitation I say, "I'll take a beer," Mr. Giles has never seen me drink.

"What about you, good looking?" the waitress flirts with Mr. Giles.

"A rum and coke," he replies.

The waitress rewards Mr. Giles with a wink, and a little sway in her hips as she walks away. She should not have bothered, because he has already turned back to me. Now, I am ready to tell him everything: about the hard work of basic training, the prejudice from the white soldiers, the rifle drills, Pit and Sgt. Moses, digging holes, the fight at the excavation site, Georgette, and the Freedom Band.

I pause for a moment to put a nickel in the jukebox, punch the button for *Take the A Train,* and I get a thumbs up from Mr. Giles. We both stop talking when the waitress brings our food to the table. We each have a big serving of very tender pork broken into small chunks and covered with a tangy red sauce.

The corn on the cob is drenched in oleomargarine, and the slaw prepared with lots of sweet pickles. The waitress brings an extra plate holding what must be a half pan of cornbread. We wave off more drinks, and dig into our feast. After five minutes, Mr. Giles lifts his head from his plate, takes a long drink of water, and sips his rum and coke.

"Man, that's some good food, LeRoy."

I nod then realize he is ready to talk more. He asks how it feels to sleep in a barracks, and if I get along with my fellow soldiers. He asks many questions about the fight I had three months ago, and the reaction of the brass to the trouble on base. He tells me he's read about these conflicts between the races on military bases all across the country, and he wonders if America will ever be the same after the war. We talk about the Double V campaign, and he tells me a great deal more about it than I'd already heard.

We finish our meal, order another round of drinks and begin to talk about music. We take turns feeding the jukebox which is up to date on all the popular songs. We listen to Ella and Benny, Cab and Lena and all the big bands. After a time I show him my new compositions.

"This is very nice, son."

Mr. Giles has called me son before, and I always felt uneasy about it. I admire him and his musicianship, and he is a great teacher, but he is nothing like my father. He is the kind of man Pit would give a hard time. Maybe not to his face, but behind his back he would call him a "pansy," or "sweet." Mr. Giles wouldn't stand a chance as a recruit under Sgt. Moses. I smile at the idea, and Mr. Giles thinks I am reacting to his praise.

"I mean it, these arrangements are very sophisticated. The trumpet and piano piece is really lovely. You've certainly learned a great deal since I saw you last."

"Thanks."

I feel my face begin to flush. Sweet or not, Mr. Giles means a lot to me and I soak in his praise, like the pork on our plates drawing up that delicious barbeque sauce.

Chapter 24

(Georgette)

I know Boone wonders why I haven't called. I'm not as decisive as he is. When I have a choice to make, it can take days, even weeks, for me to see things clearly. The only thing I've been absolutely sure about of late is joining the Army; about that I have no regrets. But now I have a decision that will change the rest of my life and I feel very confused. If I make a commitment to Boone I will finish out my tour of duty and go back to Pender to plan for his return, and our marriage. After the war, Boone might decide to become a mechanic, but there will be tremendous pressure for him to return to his farm. If that happens, I'll be a farm wife. But, if I marry LeRoy, it will be a whole new way of life.

"Boone or LeRoy?" I ask myself aloud.

"What did you say, Georgette?"

Clarice's question startles me. I didn't hear her return to our section of the personnel building. Sunlight pours through the gigantic windows of the single floor facility which is the size of an airplane hangar. In the two front corners of the building ten offices provide privacy for the officers who oversee the clerical units. In the middle of the building, five dozen wood desks and chairs are grouped in an open area to provide workspace for the

WAAC enlistees. In the rear is the windowless file area cordoned off by a floor-to-ceiling wire fence.

It is just past midday, and the air in the building is stifling. The girls will be returning from the mess hall to work another five hours, but I've opted to remain at my desk because my stomach is too unsettled to eat. Clarice puts her courier bag into the drawer of her desk and places a large stack of files on top. We are still processing dozens and dozens of deployment orders. We've all heard rumors about the war turning because of some secret new weapon, so we are handling papers at a faster pace. The good news is even more Negro troops are being shipped out.

"Did you say something about LeRoy?" Clarice inquires, already sorting through the new files. "Is he okay? He must be getting nervous about performing in New York City and Washington, DC."

"Uh, yeah he's excited about the trip, but I don't think he's nervous. He's always very...mellow."

"That's true. He is one smooth dude. Mysterious too, like those jazz guys. He doesn't wear the dark glasses like they do, but his eyes don't show much anyway."

"Clarice, I need to talk to you."

I'm hoping we'll be alone in the bullpen a few more minutes. Clarice comes over to sit at the chair next to my desk.

"What is it? You still worried about Boone's letter?"

185

"He and I have talked about getting married since high school so I know he means this," I place my hand on Boone's letter.

"Has LeRoy asked you to wait?"

"No, but I think he will. We have a date tonight. He says he wants to talk to me about something important."

"Well, you know I like LeRoy," Clarice begins slowly. "He's a real gentleman. But what I want to know Georgette, is do you love him?" She looks me right in the eye.

"Of course I love him."

"I just wondered. I know the two of you talk all the time about not wanting to go back to the country, and about city life. I've wondered a few times if you love LeRoy, or just the idea of doing something new?"

I never give Clarice enough credit. When Loretta and I spend time with Pit and LeRoy, Clarice sometimes tags along. It must be awkward for her, but she doesn't seem to mind. She is a good sport and knows how to mix with lots of people and make her own fun. She's also very observant, and has proven it many times.

"Georgette, when you talk about LeRoy, you act like you have a schoolgirl crush. But when you speak of Boone, the way you look is more like...like you admire him, like he's some kind of hero."

We see Mae and Glory come in the front door and head over to the desk pool, so Clarice rises from my side chair and returns to her own desk. I rush my next words to her.

"But I want a boyfriend, not a hero. Heroes aren't dreamy." I laugh, and so does Clarice.

"Who's dreamy?" Mae says with a big smile, and an unanswered question.

Chapter 25

(Pit/Georgette)

"So, what are you telling me Georgette? You mean Moses had to leave his last assignment because he's a sissy?"

"That's not what I said, Pit. The clerk at Fort Meyer said it was just a rumor. But, it looks like maybe he was transferred so he would have a clean file."

"I can't believe my ears. That mean little son-of-a-bitch is a sissy, and to think I've been scared of him. He marches around like he is regular Army and some big shot, but he ain't even a real man."

There is a light wind and the dust is swirling around my ankles giving the desert a hazy, white color. Waves of heat rise from the engine of Georgette's Jeep but I'm already hot.

"Pit, did you hear what I said? It's just a rumor." Georgette's voice cuts through my thoughts.

"Yes, I hear you, I hear you." I am so angry I can feel my heart pounding in my ears, and a rust taste forms in my mouth.

"Do you know he called me a nigger, Georgette? My first day on this base and he treated me like I was nothing, and all the time that motherfucker..."

"Please Pit, watch you language."

"I apologize. It's just that..."

"Pit, you know you can't tell anyone. I mean it. If you do, I'll get in trouble." Georgette's hands are moving nervously back and forth around the steering wheel.

"I wasn't supposed to be reading Sgt. Moses' file in the first place. I was just filing his furlough papers, and saw his record of transfer from Florida, but it wasn't complete so I decided to call Katie Mae at Ft. Meyer."

Georgette tries to explain all the details to me, but I don't care about any of it.

"Okay, okay, but we have to tell LeRoy. He's got to know about this so he can watch out for himself. Moses has him fooled. He had us all fooled."

"LeRoy is away for the day…and I couldn't keep this under my hat, so that's why I told you but please, Pit, you can't let anyone else know. You have to promise me,"

Georgette is so upset that I decide to give her my promise, but I have no intention of keeping it.

"I'll tell LeRoy tonight when I see him. Ok?" Georgette leans towards me. I hang the shovel over my shoulder but don't respond.

"What are you thinking, Pit?" she asks nervously.

"I'm thinking this whole join the army and be a man stuff, is just a bunch of crap."

I should have kept what I learned to myself. But I saw Pit standing near the edge of the road and I couldn't help myself. What was I thinking?

These kinds of rumors are all you need in the Army to make or break a man, or a woman for that matter. There are dozens of WAACS trying to hide the fact that they are mannish, even though they stick out like a coffee pot in a tea cozy. But, as long as they do their work, and keep to their own kind, nobody much cares. It's different for the men. A male soldier who fools around with other men just isn't tolerated. I've processed the papers of a few soldiers who were discharged for what was called 'undesirable behavior'. The brass has even been known to cover up acts of violence against homosexual soldiers. In the long run, these men are better off leaving the army before they get hurt, or worse, at the hands of other soldiers.

I don't understand what would make a man prefer another man over a woman, but God had made us all, and some of us he made different— smart or tall, left handed or buck-toothed, sometimes with special talents or just the ambition to be somebody important. But, in the army it is discouraged to draw attention to yourself. The army is not about individuality, the purpose of boot camp is to change individuals into members of a group ready to follow orders.

If the report about Sergeant Moses is true, he certainly has been cautious here at Huachuca. None of us would have suspected that this buttoned down, by the book, hard-driving man is anything but what he seems. By all accounts, he's an excellent soldier and it would be a shame if his career is hurt just because he is different.

And there is also race to think of. Despite his harshness towards colored soldiers, Moses has proven he is one of us. At Huachuca, rumors take no heed of rank, record or color, they grow like those sticky desert bushes surrounding the base— rolling with the wind, picking up loose debris, and becoming larger and larger as they travel along the sand.

I don't trust Pit's promise. I believe he will use what I've confided, to embarrass LeRoy and get even with Sgt. Moses. I think of what my mama would say about the situation I've made. "It's not a good idea to say everything you think, or to tell everything you know, Sis." She has said this to me more times than I care to count. I believe in speaking my mind but it has so often put me at odds with friends and family, especially with my father. This is one of the times I should have held my own counsel, mama's words for keeping my mouth shut.

Chapter 26

(LeRoy)

Mr. Giles and I have had a wonderful afternoon. We've laughed and drank, something we'd never done back at home, and we've talked for hours about music. He made suggestions about my compositions, scribbling notations on the sheet music—each mark making the piece better.

The waitress comes over from time to time to see if we need anything, really to see if Mr. Giles needs anything, and he gives her one of his big smiles on every visit. After many hours and several drinks, she brings two big cups of hot coffee and a couple of thin slices of homemade apple pie made with real sugar and butter, a rarity in war times.

"On the house," she announces with a twinkle in her eye for me, and a sultry look for Mr. Giles. He responds by offering his hand, and when she takes it, kisses the back of hers.

"Thank you, my dear, you're charming," he tells her.

She leaves the table floating on cloud nine. Pit would be surprised to know Mr. Giles has a way with women equal to his own.

We are both shocked when Mr. Giles looks at his watch and realizes there is only a half hour before I have to board the bus for my return to the base.

"Where does the time go, LeRoy," he says more than asks.

I suddenly feel sad. These hours have taken me back to the best parts of home. I miss this man who has taught me so much about music and believes in my talent and I miss being connected to something that is not about being a soldier. Music is more than military parades and ceremonies. Music is about beauty, and life, and being human. In the last year, I'd almost forgotten that.

"Mr. Giles," I begin, finding myself choked with emotion. "Sometimes I just want to be away from the army. I walk around angry a lot of the time. They hate us here, and when you see and feel that every day you begin to hate yourself. Home wasn't perfect, but being a soldier isn't what I want either."

My teacher doesn't say a word, and his eyes encourage me to continue. I take a long drink of water. There are things I want to talk about that I can't share with anyone, not even Georgie.

"Some of the guys love being here because they can do all the things they couldn't do at home. They walk around acting all puffed up, and swearing and drinking and womanizing, and they talk a lot about wanting to go to the front lines to fight."

"Don't you have friends here, LeRoy? Your letters mention a buddy you call Pit, I believe, and the new band must give you lots of opportunity to meet others who are serious about music."

"Yes, that helps some," I admit.

193

"Tell me about your girlfriend? What's her name, Georgette?"

"Georgie, I call her Georgie," I smile thinking of her.

"What is she like?" Mr. Giles asks with interest.

"She understands me, I think. Or at least she understands why I needed to leave home. She's not like other girls, she doesn't mind that I'm not some ladies' man, and she likes how I play."

Mr. Giles stares right at me. He has a kind of faraway look in his eyes as he listens, but now focuses them on me.

"Do you love her, LeRoy?"

"I think I do."

"Have you been in love before?"

"I'm not sure. What does it feel like?"

He doesn't answer right away. He picks up his glass, and drains the last bit of rum and coke.

"It's bittersweet. It makes your heart ache sometimes, but other times you think you can conquer the world. It is an exhilaration that begins in your chest and reaches out to your head and feet." He lifts his glass again but finds it empty. "I think I might know something about what you're going through, LeRoy. I believe you will find your way to what is right for you."

His explanation of being in love doesn't help me much, and I'm struggling to keep my sadness from spilling over. I've had too much to drink. My eyes blur with tears, so I focus them on the red and white squares of the tablecloth. I only look up when the waitress returns to our table.

"Here's your bill, sugar," she is saying to Mr. Giles. He must have signaled for it, and neither seems to notice as I swipe at my eyes.

"And here you are young lady," he says handing her several bills, and gesturing for me to put my money away.

"Thank you, gentlemen," the waitress says in a way that tells me the tip is generous, followed by, "and I hope you both come again…anytime." I am included in this hope because of my meal companion.

Mr. Giles and I gather up our things and put on our coats as we head to the door. I have fifteen minutes to catch my bus. It has become quite cold, so we pull up our collars when we pause outside.

"LeRoy, go on to your bus. I believe you said the boarding house is just up the street, and I'll find my way. It's so good to see you, son, and this was the best afternoon I've had in a long time."

He holds out his hand and I shake it firmly.

"Do you still have the stamps and envelopes I gave you?"

I nod yes.

"I expect you to write me a bit more often, okay?"

I smile, feeling like his shy pupil again. "Yes sir."

He walks away quickly, turning back to wave when I call out: "thanks for everything, Mr. Giles."

I turn toward downtown and in the distance, I see the bus just coming to rest across from the station. Several soldiers get off, along with a few civilians who work or volunteer at the base. I stop short when I see Sergeant Moses step down from the bus. He is wearing his dress greens, carries a suitcase, and has an overcoat across his arm. He walks briskly toward the station main entrance, stops to put on his overcoat, and then continues past the station heading in my direction. He doesn't see me, and I'm not sure why, but I don't want him to, so I duck into the door nearest me.

"What can I do for you solider?"

I've entered an office that sells war bonds, and issues ration cards. The woman asking the question is small, white and afraid of me. We look at each other for a few moments. Behind her are several other women staring at me from their desks.

"Nothing ma'am, sorry ma'am," I blurt.

I look through the window to make sure it is all clear, and step out of the office. Moses has passed my hiding place, and I walk quickly to the bus. I peek over my shoulder to see that he has crossed the street and is walking with a purpose. When he asked me this morning about my own day pass he didn't mention he was also coming to town. Of course, he has no reason to tell me of his comings and goings.

196

I move straight to the back rows of the bus. I see a few familiar faces but I want to sit alone. Something nags at me. The Sarge was carrying a suitcase, I guess he needs a few days off before we head overseas. Most of the guys in the band are getting passes for a quick trip home or to have a week of fun before our travel. But, the Sergeant didn't go into the train station. He headed for the colored part of town where I'd just come from. Maybe he is getting some food before he gets on the train. The colored porters take good care of Negro troops, but train food isn't nearly as good as Kenny's, or some of the other places in town.

It's a good idea for the Sarge to get some rest and recreation before we ship out, because there won't be much time for relaxing during our deployment. The Freedom Band is considered a special duty unit and the Sarge will be under close scrutiny by the brass to make sure his colored troops toe the line. When we visit Washington, DC and New York City, the colored and white band members will stay in separate hotels and if we ride a train, the Negro members will be seated in the rear cars. I tense up thinking about how unfair this all seems, and I imagine it is even harder for the sergeant. He was heard to say he doesn't like babysitting a bunch of musicians, and would rather be training soldiers for the infantry. But sometimes, after band practice, when we are just fooling around with a jazz piece, he closes his eyes and smiles when he listens. More than a few times he's nodded his approval when I've sent my trumpet soaring over the top of a melody. He isn't such a bad egg.

The bus pulls away from the curb for the trip back to Fort Huachuca. I settle into the seat, no longer troubled by seeing Sgt. Moses. Instead, I try to concentrate on what I'll say to Georgie tonight.

Chapter 27

(Georgette/LeRoy)

LeRoy doesn't respond at all when I tell him about Sgt. Moses. We sit at a booth in the tavern. He has paid for beef sandwiches, pickles, and a couple of cokes but he isn't eating. I can tell he's thinking about what I've said, but he doesn't say a word, he just stares at his food. The jukebox blasts music, and some of the guys and girls are jitterbugging. At the back of the room I see a group crouching around what I'm sure is an illegal crap game. I glance at the door to spot the informal sentry the dice players post in case MPs head toward the tavern. When I return my attention to LeRoy, he is still lost in thought, so I break the silence.

"Pit got angry when I told him. I feel real bad that I didn't just keep what I heard to myself, but I had to tell somebody, and..."

"You told Pit?" Leroy's head jerks up violently, his tone is harsh.

"Well, yes...that's what I was saying. I had to tell somebody and I thought the girls in the office might spread it all over the base."

"And you think Pit won't?" Leroy asks raising his voice.

"Well, I just wasn't thinking. You weren't around, and I saw Pit at his work detail so I mentioned it to him," I say defensively. "LeRoy, I made him promise that he won't tell anyone else."

I'm sure my voice reveals more doubt than conviction.

After a moment, LeRoy reaches over and touches my arm. "I know you didn't mean any harm, Georgie," his voice softens, "but this kind of gossip is dangerous."

"I know," I say hanging my head.

LeRoy pats my arm, smiles, and tries to take the conversation in a different direction. "I saw Sergeant Moses in town this afternoon."

"Oh, really? I guess he was leaving for his furlough. Sgt. Banks is filling in for him with the band while he's on leave."

"Georgie, isn't Moses from Chicago?" LeRoy looks deeply into my eyes.

"Uh-huh. Master Sergeant, Robert Moses, born in Chicago, Illinois in 1905. Enlisted in the army in 1924," I recite from memory.

LeRoy stares at his sandwich again. When he works on a new piece of music he says it's like putting together a jigsaw puzzle. He has that look of concentration now. We pass a few more minutes in silence and I nibble on my sandwich.

"Didn't you say you wanted to talk to me about something?"

"Huh?" LeRoy looks blankly at me.

"You said there was something you wanted to talk about, LeRoy."

My voice has a bit of an edge. I feel ignored. LeRoy has completely forgotten we are on a date. In just a matter of weeks he'll be far away from Fort Huachuca; the time we have left should be precious to him, as it is to me. LeRoy sees the set of my jaw and tries to take my hand, but I pull it away.

"Aw Georgie, don't be mad. I'm just caught up in my thoughts."

"Like always," I say pouting.

I believe LeRoy would have told me nothing about the puzzle he's been piecing together, but he starts talking to lift the cloud hanging over our table.

"Georgie, I think I've figured out something. It all fits."

"What fits?" my curiosity chases down, and sprints past, my hurt feelings.

LeRoy leans across the table, puts his hand on my arm, and lowers his voice.

"I think Sergeant Moses' furlough is to be with my teacher, Mr. Giles."

Pit makes a beeline for me and Georgie when we come out of the tavern. He must have been waiting for us.

"Did Georgette tell you, LeRoy?" he says with the excitement of a hound dog on the scent of a scampering rabbit.

"Yes, she did Pit. I hope you haven't told anybody, because we don't know for sure if it's true...and you know what will happen if..."

"Man, the Sarge is a sissy!" he spits out the statement.

We are all three silent for a moment, and I look around to see if anyone has overheard.

"Pit, man, all I'm saying is if these honky soldiers get wind of the rumors they'll have something else to use against us."

"Are you saying, it's okay that Moses is sweet? Is that what you're saying?" Pit's eyes are narrow and questioning.

"No, that's not what I'm saying, but we don't need to drag the Sarge down. If it was rumors about you, or any of the guys, I'd say the same thing."

"What do you mean if it was about me? Boy, you know better than to say that shit," Pit's words and tone are threats, and he steps towards me. "Are you out of your mind?"

Georgette steps between us, and puts her hands on Pit's chest.

"All LeRoy is saying is that we have to stick up for each other. Besides, the rumor might not even be true."

Pit looks hard at me, and then at Georgette. I see Pit's shoulders relax a bit, and I'm relieved he isn't going to hit me.

"You know it's true." Pit speaks to Georgie but stares at me, then brushes roughly against my arm as he leaves us to walk up the road towards the barracks.

202

"LeRoy, what should we do?" Georgette asks.

"There's nothing for us to do, except speak up for the Sarge when we have the chance."

I don't tell Georgie what I'm really thinking. Pit is going to make trouble for Moses. If the Sarge is hurt, Mr. Giles will also be hurt. I can't stand the thought of that. Realizing the tie between these two men doesn't make me angry or shocked; I'm just curious. Mr. Giles doesn't have a mean bone in his body, but Sergeant Moses can be very mean, he's shown that in his treatment of Pit. The two men seem so different, like a duet between a piccolo and a bass guitar. I wonder how they can blend, and the thought stirs me.

I know very little about sex. I laugh and nod when the guys talk about women late at night in the barracks, or when we sit over beers in the tavern, but their vulgar remarks usually make me uncomfortable. I know for sure that I get sex feelings when I hold Georgie close, and when I kiss her. But, I have to admit, I've had those same feelings around some men. I had them the time Butch and I wrestled in my backyard and he pinned me to the ground.

"Do you give, LeRoy? You give?" Butch had demanded. I made one last effort to wriggle free from his weight, and my growing erection embarrassed me.

"I give up. Let go of me," I shouted.

203

When Butch released me, I sat in the dirt, my knees to my chest, for a couple of minutes until my body obeyed my orders.

And there is a more recent example, with Pit. Our unit was digging holes as usual, this time for a new landfill at the edge of the base. Someone said something funny and Pit, bare-chested, threw his head back with laughter, the sweat gleaming on his bulging muscles. As I watched, the hair on the back of my neck stood on end like the sharp needles of a desert cactus, and I had to shovel dirt furiously to recover myself.

Over the years, I've come to think of these feelings as the music inside me. I sense music in the things around me all the time. Not just in the singing of birds, or the rhythm of a passing freight train, but at odd times, like when I take the first bite of a mango, or when I feel the smoothness of a piece of wood. Only now am I beginning to understand that maybe these sensations are also connected to sex.

Georgie is staring at me. I quickly look away, in case she can somehow read my mind. She puts her hand on my arm and then slides it into my hand. We don't say much as we walk back to the main area of the camp, and then to the women's barracks.

"Georgie, I want to be with you. I love you, and I want us to be together."

"I love you," she says.

"Can we go away for a few days, just the two of us? Maybe we could take a bus to Albuquerque and see the Rio Grande."

"I need to give it some thought, LeRoy."

I am sure of Georgie. She is the one thing in my life I know won't betray me. I pull her close, my arms tight around her small waist. When she lifts her head, I give her a deep, wet kiss. I feel her body give way, and the racing of her heart. Suddenly, she drops from her tiptoes and pushes me away.

"LeRoy, I can't catch my breath."

I try to draw her back to me. I can feel the music swell, but Georgie stands her ground.

"We'll be together soon, LeRoy. It's almost curfew so let's say goodnight."

"You mean you *will* go away with me?"

She nods 'yes.'

I have to double time it to my barracks before the bed count. It has been quite a day...first my visit with Mr. Giles, solving the puzzle about Giles and Sgt. Moses, the confrontation with Pit, admitting my feelings for certain men, and now my longing for Georgie.

The run in the cool night air clears my mind of these overlapping thoughts. I think the only one who can help me make sense of all this is Mr. Giles. I'll call him when he returns from Mexico.

Sgt. Banks is standing near my cot when I burst into the barracks, banging the door so hard it hits the wall. Most of the guys are already in bed, reading or smoking. A few are sitting at the table writing letters or playing a last hand of cards.

"You cut it kind of close, Dowdell," Banks says making a mark on his clipboard.

"Yes sergeant. It's been a hell of a day."

I put my bag beneath my cot, flop hard onto the wool blanket and begin unlacing my shoes. Banks looks at me with no apparent interest in my remark. "Lights out in ten minutes, Dowdell."

Chapter 28

(Sgt. Moses)

It's been two years since I've seen Bonnie (I refuse to call him Bonaparte). It's too long for sweethearts to be apart. I'm envious of the soldiers who can pin pictures of their wives or girlfriends over their cots, or in their footlockers. I have two small photos of Bonnie, but they're discretely tucked in a book on Army regulations, and if anyone would ever see them I'd just say he's my kid brother. We're careful in our letters to make them appear to be between a man and a woman, and our phone calls are infrequent because they don't afford us much privacy.

I'm excited at the prospect of our reunion. I've arranged for adjoining rooms at the boarding house, so when I arrive, I sign the lobby book and quickly climb the three flights of stairs to my room. I toss my suitcase and overcoat onto the bed, and check myself in the mirror. Then, I lean close to the connecting door and whistle the first four notes of Beethoven's Fifth Symphony. After just a moment, the next four notes come from the other side—our signal that the coast is clear.

Bonnie flings open the door and, as usual, I am taken aback by his beauty. I step into his embrace and we hold each other for a long time, the smell of his aftershave sends a tingle through my loins. I push him back to arm's length, holding both his hands, and we stare at each other without speaking. We close the distance again and share a kiss that makes up for lost time.

He has made the room ready for our lovemaking. A bottle of red wine breathes on the dresser and next to it are two stemmed glasses. The bed is turned down, and rose petals sprinkled on the pillows. The room's radio is set to a station that plays jazz standards and a sheer, burgundy scarf is draped over the lampshade giving the room a muted ambience.

"How did you manage to bring all this stuff on the train?" I ask. How did you keep rose petals fresh all the way, from Georgia?"

"You know how resourceful I am," he says flirtatiously.

I kiss him again, and our hands find each other.

"I've missed you more than you know, Bonnie."

"I can tell," he whispers.

I turn up the volume on the radio to cover the sounds of our passion, and allow the pressures of war, fear of discovery, and prejudice melt away.

Chapter 29

(Georgette)

LeRoy has a three-day furlough, and I've also put in my request for time off. He says when he goes overseas, he wants to have lots of memories of the two of us to keep him strong. Even as LeRoy pours out these words, I think of Boone.

Boone and I have loved each other a long time, and we've both been tempted to go beyond petting but we've been raised to believe sex is for the marriage bed. Now I am about to give myself to a boy I've known, and loved, for only a few months.

I've watched intently in the dark of a movie house balcony as a beautiful woman on the screen is swept off her feet by the promises of a handsome man. The romance begins with a feverish kiss, then the picture blurs or moves off to a moonlit sky and our imaginations take us to some forbidden, but urgent, act of love.

I can't imagine that kind of love affair with Boone. He is a country boy, large and muscular, his hands and voice rough. He walks with long strides and a heavy step. Boone would be out of place at a theater or symphony.

LeRoy is more like the man in the movie-version romance. His voice is soft and mellow, with a slender body that moves gracefully whether walking, or on a dance floor. I can picture LeRoy in a tuxedo.

I'm no longer Georgette from Pender County. I'm Georgie, modern and independent, ready to take another step closer to the woman I've dreamed I can be. I will go away with LeRoy, and when the war is over he and I will marry, and live and work in the city. I'll call Boone and let him know of my decision—he'll understand. He'll have a demanding job with the Tuskegee airmen, and will soon forget about me. When he returns to Pender, he'll find another girl to marry, maybe LuAnn Briscoe.

We live in new times, LeRoy, Boone and I. We won't ever be able to return to the normal we knew before the war.

Chapter 30

(Sgt. Moses)

I returned to Huachuca late last night, and this morning I am
still caught up in the wonder and release of my week with
Bonnie. I rarely have the luxury of letting down my guard, but
with him it is safe to talk about my feelings, and shed tears for
the indignities I've endured. He rocked me in his arms as I let
my emotions flow, and he said all the things I needed to hear.

"Robert, you're an exceptional soldier. The brass knows it
and one day the recruits will understand what you've tried to do
for them. You've put your heart into this work. That's who you
are, and I don't ever want you to change," he said to me.

Bonnie has his own cross to bear. When his mother
became ill, he didn't hesitate to set aside his life in Chicago and
return to Americus to become her primary caretaker. He is a
world-class pianist and composer, but for the last three years his
considerable talents have only been on display at a small rural
church, and a Negro secondary school. This lifestyle change has
been difficult on our relationship. He no longer has the time, or
the money, to hop on a train to meet me when I have a furlough,
so I was relieved when he set aside his insistence on equity, to
let me pay for our trip.

The day after our sweet reunion at the boarding house, we
traveled by bus to a beautiful port town in Sonora, Mexico. For

five days we lounged on the beach in the early morning sun watching the local fishermen take their boats out with empty nets, and return hours later with a full catch of shrimp.

In the afternoons, we explored the small shops filled with beautiful, handmade crafts painted in brilliant oranges, yellows and blues. At night, we ate wonderful seafood and rice dishes with olives, peppers and blue corn tortillas, at outdoor cafes. We drank lots of red wine and tequila with the patrons at one or another of the cafes that lined the village, and enjoyed the twinkling of the wharf lights in the black water.

We were temporary exiles from a war that held countries on several continents in its grip. We spoke of music and art, we learned of the weather's impact on the pristine coastline, and we showed appreciation for photos of beautiful, brown children and smiling sweethearts with flashing eyes and long, dark hair. Rarely did the talk turn to the fighting in the world, but we often discussed race and prejudice. These villagers, with proximity to the U.S. border, knew that color and class made a difference, and they had witnessed the treatment of America's black citizens with their own eyes and hearts.

Mexico had inherited the Spanish caste system imposing inferiority on Mestizos, a legacy still felt in the preferential treatment afforded those with light skin tones, rather than dark. But, these residents still couldn't understand how Americans, freed of servitude in a Civil War, continued to be treated like slaves.

Our friendly conversations lasted long into the evenings, and when the cafés closed, Bonnie and I returned to our love nest slightly drunken and filled with goodwill. No one held questions in their eyes about two men traveling together and sharing a small apartment with one bed, we were simply accepted. I will always remember those wonderful, relaxing times and generous people, with deep gratitude and affection.

There had been only a single, tense moment during our blissful vacation. One morning we brought in the dawn with lovemaking and afterwards lay exhausted in our tousled sheets. Bonnie's head rested against my outstretched arm, and he brought up the subject of PFC Dowdell.

"I didn't tell you about my visit with LeRoy, did I?"

"Oh, you mean, PFC Dowdell. No you didn't. How did it go?"

I feigned interest in this pillow talk but, honestly, I preferred to study the place where his curly hair met the top of his ear.

"LeRoy and I had a wonderful time. We listened to music, ate, and talked for hours. We even had a couple of drinks. Robert, he showed me a few of his compositions, and believe me, he's a very talented boy."

"He's no boy, Bonnie. He's a man and a soldier."

"I know he's a man now, I could see the changes in him, but I'll always think of him as my student. I had to stop myself from protesting when he ordered a beer. In Americus he was like a fish out of water, but he seems to be finding his way now—even if it did mean putting on a uniform."

I couldn't resist challenging him on the last point, and I withdrew my arm. "Giles, what do you have against my job?" I resented his jabs at the army, and I wasn't happy that our time together had turned into a discussion about one of my recruits.

"So, no more Bonnie, huh?" he said perching on his elbow.

I didn't respond.

I've told you before, Robert, I think the army has treated you like a gold-digging mistress," he said matter-of-factly. "She uses you for what you can give, and you keep giving, because you think one day she'll love you."

That was the final straw and I sat up, swinging my legs to the floor and turning my back to him. Bonnie left the bed and closed the bathroom door behind him. I lit a Chesterfield watching it glow orange, and feeling my anger subside with each inhale and exhale of smoke. When Bonnie returned, I was over being mad. I extended my arm as an invitation. He crawled into bed, leaned close against me, and I lowered my head to meet his tongue.

"I'm sorry I didn't give you a chance to finish telling me about Dowdell, but I don't want to talk about work first thing in the morning."

"You don't think of your men as just work, do you?"

"Of course I do. That *is* my work, turning them into soldiers."

"I guess I never thought of it that way. I thought you were, you know, guiding them through all the hurt they have to take, and defending them to the top brass."

"No Bonnie, that's *not* my job."

"Well, I sure hope you're looking out for LeRoy. You know you promised."

"I said I'd keep an eye on him, and I have been. You don't have a crush on this kid, do you?" I asked half-jokingly.

"I like him, Robert. He reminds me of me when I was his age, that's all."

"Do you think he's family?" I asked using the code word.

"I don't know. He could be. He's questioning his feelings about a woman he knows. I told him he'd find someone who's right for him."

I nodded, and we were silent for a long time. Then Bonnie changed the subject with a question, and a gentle tug of my chest hair.

"So what should we do with our last two days in paradise?"

Chapter 31

(LeRoy)

I've picked out an engagement gift for Georgie. I couldn't afford a ring, but I wanted to give her something she could wear with pride. I bought it at the base PX with the help of Clarice, who wasn't all that eager to assist me at first, but finally came around.

"LeRoy, why do you need me to help you pick out something for Georgette? The two of you are connected at the hip, so you should know what she likes."

"Georgie's told me many times you remind her of her sister, Barbara. She says you have good, common sense."

Clarice looked at me to see if I was sincere.

"Okay, I'll help if I can."

Sure enough, it was Clarice who spotted the ten-karat gold, genuine mother-of-pearl locket.

"This one. Georgette will like this one," she said excitedly handing me the locket.

I turned it over in my hand, "why do you think she'll like it?"

"It's delicate, pretty but not flashy, and it's classy looking. See, it opens here, and you can put a small photo inside. You could even have something engraved on the back, if you want," Clarice said.

"I think maybe one of my Freedom Band photos will look good in the locket."

"LeRoy, you really love Georgette, don't you?"

Clarice's question caught me off guard. She looked at me the way I thought Georgie's mother or father might if they were asking the question. Her stare demanded a response.

"Yes, I do. Why are you asking me that?"

"Don't take this wrong, LeRoy, but I don't think you've been with a whole lot of girls. I know you like Georgette a lot, but you don't act like you're in love with her. Not the way she's in love with you."

I didn't know whether to be hurt, or mad. I thought Clarice was butting into my business, and she had managed to stir up my own doubts again.

"You don't know what you're talking about," I finally responded.

"I don't mean any harm. It's just that Georgette is a good friend and, well, please don't mention this to her. I know you're a good guy, I've always thought that."

"No harm taken."

I always thought Clarice was a fine girl, and pretty, too. She had a way of not drawing notice to herself, but she was fun, and, Georgie was right, sensible. The woman at the PX put the locket on a sash, and wrapped the gift in a small white box with a pink bow.

"I'm gonna give this to her next Friday, before we leave for Albuquerque," I told Clarice putting the box in my pocket.

"That will be nice, LeRoy."

I confided to Pit that I was going to ask Georgie to marry me. I just kind of brought it up in conversation, I didn't want to make a big deal of it because I expected he would make fun of me, but he wasn't even interested. For the last two weeks all he could focus on was getting even with Sgt. Moses, and he'd been hard at work bad mouthing him every chance he got. Although Georgette and I have defended the Sarge, the rumor about him has firmly taken hold.

A few days ago, one of the band members made a nasty comment about Moses. We were lined up on the practice field in full uniform. Sergeant Moses had dressed down two of the colored soldiers for having mud on their new patent leather shoes, and ordered them back into the barracks to clean them while the rest of us waited 'at attention' in the hot sun. That's when a white trombonist said loud enough to be heard, "I guess the Sarge wants all his men to look pretty like him." A few guys snickered at the remark, but Sgt. Terry glared at the brass section and they settled down.

When I confronted Pit about spreading the rumors and he criticized me.

"You're just worried about your damn marching band, LeRoy," he said and stared me down. So, I backed off.

More and more I feel like an outsider with Pit, Sylvester and the others. All I want to do is fit in, but the Freedom Band, the situation with Sgt. Moses, and my own confused feelings have left me at odds with those I used to count as friends. Thank God, I still have Georgie. She says she loves me, and when I asked her why, she filled my head with all the good things I want to believe about myself.

I should be on top of the world. I'm heading off to Europe, playing and writing music every day, and a pretty girl loves me, but I'm unsettled. It might be the desert getting to me, the sand has a way of reaching out, and turning everything a desperate, gray.

I plan to phone Mr. Giles at the church on Wednesday, when he'll be there for choir practice. Maybe when I speak with him, it will calm my nerves. Maybe I'll even hint that I know about him and Sgt. Moses, and tell him that it's alright with me.

Chapter 32

(Clarice)

I really adore Georgette and Loretta, they're my best friends. I hadn't imagined finding other women I'd feel so close to when I joined the army. We're all part of a group of friends, but to tell the truth I'm sick of being the confidante, the pal and the girl with the common sense. I want to be someone's one-and-only. I'd fooled myself once into believing I had that status when I was a career girl in Birmingham, but my lover wouldn't leave his wife. That's why I joined the army, so I could get as far away as possible from the source of my hurt pride.

I'd completed course work at the O'Connor Business School, and could do accounting, type 85-words per minute, and take shorthand. Those skills got me a full-time job as bookkeeper at the Brooks Insurance Agency. Fred Burghardt Williams noticed my acumen right away. He was the agency's top salesman and a natural people person—charming to the ladies, buddy to the men, and a pied piper to children. When he walked in a door, people smiled without realizing it.

"Who do we have here?" He locked his eyes on me as he queried Mr. Dawson the agency manager.

"That's our new accountant, F.B. She's fresh out of business school and comes highly recommended." Dawson said. "Clarice Watkins, meet F.B. Williams."

He took my hand, looked me deeply in the eyes, and my whole twenty-one years of life flashed through my mind. I was too naïve to know he was pure danger.

"Why, I can see that she is both fresh, and highly recommended, Mr. Dawson," F.B. said with no shame.

I blushed and said: "I've seen your name in the ledger Mr. Williams, nice to meet you."

"My associates call me F.B. but you can call me Freddy."

The girls at the insurance company warned me about him. He was married, but flirted with every woman he met. He had two children—a boy three-years-old, and a baby daughter, and he kept a framed picture of his wife and two kids displayed on his desk. Everyone in town, including Mrs. Williams, knew he had other women from time to time, but he liked being married.

All the warnings, and the daily glances at that photograph on his desk, didn't stop me from beginning an affair with Freddy, or falling in love with him. Our eighteen-month relationship came to an end, when I asked him to divorce his wife so he could marry me.

"Clarice, be reasonable. I told you at the beginning, I was devoted to my wife. I just want you and me to keep on having a good time. You said you understood."

221

"I know, Freddy, but you said you loved me, and I thought that changed things. After all, you spend almost every evening at my place. It already feels like we're married."

"But Clarice, I also leave you every night to go home to my family, so I can start each day with them," he said this while putting on his shoes, and gathering his jacket. "That's what being married is, starting the day with someone. I would *never* leave my wife and kids," he spoke very plainly. He picked up his briefcase filled with insurance brochures and policy forms, and left my apartment for the last time.

I am almost over Freddy. He sent one letter right after I left Birmingham, inquiring about my wellbeing, but I never replied— afraid I might get caught up in that whirlwind again. So now my social life is as the gal pal, the friend and advisor, but never the beloved.

I could never love someone like Pit, he is a womanizer like Freddy, but also crude and immature. He's okay for a few laughs but could never be taken seriously, and I'm sure Loretta will realize this before too long. LeRoy, on the other hand, is intriguing. He's a young guy, but his soul is old. I think it must be this quality that attracts Georgette. He may not know much about pleasing a woman, but I'm betting he would be a quick study, and I wouldn't mind teaching him.

I guess I'm not much of a friend to have these thoughts about LeRoy. He and Georgette are about to become engaged so I better start looking for my own man. All I know is, I don't want to be the fifth-wheel anymore, and I'm almost over Freddy.

Chapter 33

(Boone)

Something is wrong, Lil hasn't phoned at all. She must have received my letter by now. Maybe she has found someone else and doesn't want to wait for me. Maybe she doesn't love me anymore.

Mama suggested I send a telegram and ask her to call, but telegrams during war time usually contain bad news. Now that we are three years into the war, those being drafted are sent directly to their assignments and at the end of the month I am to report to duty at Selfridge Field near Detroit. But, I need to talk to Lil before I go.

Since she won't call me, maybe I'll have to go to her. I've already been issued a uniform and dog tags which allow me to ride the train for free. I'll need only enough money for my meals, and to take Lil out on the town when I get to Tucson. It will take three days to get to Arizona, and three days to get back, so I have just enough time to take this trip. I don't know if I can even set foot on Fort Huachuca, but I'm going to try.

I tell mama of my decision, and then go out to the porch to tell Pops. He is relaxing, leaning back in a chair against the front wall of the house. He has one work-booted foot on the floor and the other dangles over his knee, his pipe hangs from the corner of his mouth, and his straw hat is pulled over his eyes.

He lifts the brim of his hat with the pipe stem when he hears me open the screen door. He has finally accepted that I won't be around to help with the farming and has been telling his friends how proud he is of me.

"Hey Pops, you think it's going to rain?" I cross over to him and sit on the porch rail.

"I can smell it coming," he says looking out to the rows of waist-high corn.

"Yeah I can, too."

"What is it, son? You nervous about putting on that uniform?"

"No, I'm not really too worried about that. There's something else."

He takes a long draw on his pipe, and waits for me to say more.

"I need to go see Lil. You know, Georgette Newton. She's in Arizona in the army and I need to talk to her, Pops."

"You and Georgette have known each other for a long time, son. She's a sweet young lady; from a good, solid farm family, he adds."

I know what he really means. Pops doesn't like LuAnn. He thinks she's stuck up. When LuAnn comes around, he is always polite, but never stays around to engage in conversation the way he does when he likes one of my friends.

"Pops, I'm taking a train tomorrow for Arizona. I'm going to see Georgette and ask her to be my wife. I'll be gone about a week, but I'll be back home to see you and mama before I have to report for duty."

My father takes another long puff on his pipe, staring me right in the eyes, then says just two words: "God speed."

Chapter 34

(Pit)

Bennie, Sylvester, Loretta and I have talked it over. It doesn't matter what LeRoy and Georgette say, Sgt. Moses is going to get what's coming to him.

I'm not the only one who's been treated badly by Moses. The more people I tell about him being a sissy, the more stories I hear about him being high-handed, and rubbing people the wrong way. The white non-coms praise Moses to Captain Hurley because he's a career soldier, but that don't sit well with the colored non-coms. Sgt. Tyler even called me aside after roll call to tell me he wasn't a fan of Sgt. Moses.

"Private Turner, It's come to my attention that you are spreading a rumor about Sergeant Moses."

"No, Sergeant Tyler, I'm not trying to spread a rumor, I'm just telling what I heard."

"And what have you heard?"

"One of our clerks got word from Fort Meyer that Moses, uh, Sgt. Moses had to leave the base because he was, uh, fraternizing with a civilian—a white man."

"Fraternizing?" Tyler asked.

"You know, sergeant, it's disgusting to say out loud, but he's, you know, sweet."

"You know what you're saying, Turner?" Tyler's voice was very low, and his words came out as a hiss.

"It's what I was told, Sgt. Tyler."

"So, what are you going to do about it, Turner?"

"What do you mean?"

"It seems to me that these are charges of inappropriate conduct."

"Yeah, it seems not appropriate to me too," I said.

"There is a procedure for filing such charges. If you're serious about these accusations, I suggest you get your lady friend in the personnel office to provide you with the proper forms to make these charges," Tyler said.

"Well, okay, Sgt. Tyler. Uh, some of my friends think maybe we should protect Sgt. Moses because, you know, because he's colored."

"That's all well and good, Turner, but on the other hand, this kind of behavior brings disgrace to the colored units. So, if you believe what has been reported, you might want to take action to protect the honor of our troops."

Loretta helped me fill out the forms, and she promised not to tell Georgette what I was up to. When I presented the forms to Tyler for his signature, he smiled. "Private, I'll see that these papers get to Captain Hurley." He acted like it was a complete surprise to receive them.

Bennie says I was right to file the charges, but Loretta and Sylvester aren't so sure now, and Clarice thinks I'm dead wrong.

"I thought you promised Georgette you wouldn't even spread that rumor, Pit. You promised. And LeRoy wants us all to stick up for Sgt. Moses," Clarice says.

"Georgette and LeRoy can kiss my ass," I say to Clarice. I'm on my second drink.

"Man, I know you can't stand Moses, but what happens to one of us, happens to all of us. This is like helping the white man do us damage," Sylvester says.

"That's some bullshit. We ain't like the sergeant. Yeah, he colored like us but he's a sissy. That changes everything."

"Pit, would you feel the same way if Sgt. Moses hadn't been so tough on you?" Clarice asks.

All the heads at the table turn to me. I don't know how to answer that question, and I don't have to because LeRoy and Georgette come into the tavern and walk over to our table. I don't look at them.

"Hey, you two," Clarice says sounding as if we weren't just talking about them. "What are you up to?"

"We're going into town to listen to some music at the record store," LeRoy says. "You guys want to come along?"

"Don't you ever get enough of music?" I say, looking up from my drink.

229

Bennie, Sylvester and Loretta shift in their chairs, and LeRoy and Georgette give a nervous laugh. As usual, Clarice lightens things up.

"Musicians can't ever get enough music, Pit. Just like us drinkers can never get enough of this stuff," she says lifting her rum and coke.

"That's why we're always sitting here at the tavern," Sylvester adds.

Everyone laughs, but me.

Chapter 35

(Sgt. Moses)

I have been summoned to Captain Hurley's office and I know it isn't good. I got the order in person from his clerk, who arrived at the barracks before roll call. He gave me a serious look when he passed on the message. The clerks in the executive offices know everything, and are chosen for their discretion, this Corporal is no exception. I remember his supportive words to me when I'd been assigned the Freedom Band nearly three months ago and now he seems to want to say more, but he doesn't have to because his look tells me there is shit about to hit a fan that's blowing my way.

A quarter hour later, I am in the captain's waiting area. The corporal and I exchanged only a quick nod when I walk into the anteroom, and he goes directly into the captain's office to announce me, returning to busy himself with typing. I have been sitting almost ten minutes when the intercom buzzes at the corporal's desk. The corporal stands and opens the captain's door.

"You can go in now, sergeant," he says holding the door open. We exchange another hard look.

I stand at attention in front of Captain Hurley's desk, and I don't have long to wait to know what kind of trouble I have.

"How dare you give this army, and this base a bad name?" Hurley screams the question at me, his face blotching red. "Your kind should stay the hell away from the military," he continues, clearly not expecting any response to his question.

What he says next shocks me: "If I wasn't in command of this base, I'd kill you myself." Hurley stares at me with absolute disgust. I hold my ground in the middle of the room, but my jaw tightens and my legs are trembling.

"Why the hell did you join the army in the first place?" He asks looking up from what I know is my file. "I don't need this aggravation in my division and I sure as hell don't need an uppity nigger who is also a goddamn pervert."

So there it is—again. I don't know how Hurley finds out, but somehow he knows my secret. I have been very careful not to bring attention to myself at Huachuca, but Hurley knows. That's why he feels free to call me nigger because to him the other word is so, far, worse. This revelation also explains the funny looks, and wide berth I've been getting since I returned from furlough.

For nearly two minutes, there is an unholy silence in Hurley's office while he glares at me, his mouth twitching with rage. I stay at attention. A layer of sweat forms at my neck, and I feel it drip down the back of my shirt. Hurley is sizing me up, wondering how he has been fooled. Suddenly, he bangs his fist on the desk.

"You, stupid, nigger," he says each word slowly, deliberately. His voice never rises and I know it is a challenge. He wants me to react and it takes all my strength not to jump over his desk, and squeeze his pink neck until the blood vessels burst in his brain. I blink to regain composure, and a tear mingles with the sweat at the corner of my eyes. I reach way down inside to hold myself back, and hold myself up.

"Do you deny what I've said, Moses?" he finally poses an actual question.

"I'm sorry sir?" I ask in return.

"Do you deny the report I've received that you are a pervert, Moses?"

"I am not a pervert, sir." I look directly at Hurley and we both hold the stare.

Then Hurley begins to talk aloud to himself, drumming his fingers on the desk, and looking pass me.

"If it was peacetime, I'd have your ass off this base today. This damn Freedom Band is important to Colonel Murray and he doesn't need to hear anything about this."

He swivels his chair toward the window, his back to me now, and continues his rant while staring out at the desert.

"You'll be off the base in ten days and overseas for the next six months with your colored musicians. You'll be out of my hair and someone else's problem."

"May I ask who made this allegation, captain?"

Hurley spins his chair to face me. "You keep your damn mouth shut, sergeant. Do you hear me?"

"Yes sir."

A loud knock on the door momentarily breaks the tension. "What is it?" Hurley screams keeping his eyes on me. Behind me, I hear the door open and the footsteps of two people. I dare not divert my eyes from Hurley, but I hear the corporal's voice.

"Here's the man you wanted to see, captain."

I feel eyes crawling my back. In my peripheral vision PFC Turner comes to attention next to me.

"Did you make a complaint against Sgt. Moses, soldier?" Hurley says waving a piece of paper.

"Yes sir, captain."

I sense Turner glance at me. I know his friends call him Pit. I've never known why, and up to now didn't really care.

"Misconduct is a serious charge, Private Turner. Did someone put you up to this?"

"Put me up to it? I don't know what you mean, captain."

"Is this some kind of retaliation because you and the other colored soldiers think the sergeant is too tough on you?"

"I don't know about that retalayshun, captain. I'm not sure what it means, but I know what I heard about the Sarge, and that's got to be some kind of not appropriate behavior."

"Did *you* ever see him behave in the manner suggested in this complaint, private?" The captain's voice reveals his disdain for us both, now.

"Well, uh, no. I didn't really see nothing, but there's a report from Fort Meyer that says..."

"What report?" Hurley barks, leaning forward on his elbows.

"Well, not a report exactly, but one of the clerk's at Fort Meyer told PFC Newton, that Sgt. Moses was..." the captain interrupts again.

"I am not going to have the reputation of this base tarnished by hearsay, Private Turner. Is that clear?"

Hurley's tone is certainly clear to me. I doubt if Pit knows what hearsay is, but he seems to know he's lost this fight. His body sways as if hit by the wind.

"I'll be speaking to your unit leader about you, and I don't expect this matter to go any further. Do you understand me, private?"

Pit says nothing.

"I said do you understand?" Hurley shouts.

"Yes, sir," Pit also shouts, barely veiling his resentment.

"You're dismissed, Turner."

Pit salutes. Since Hurley gives no sign of returning the salute, Pit turns on his heels, and I hear the door close behind me.

The room again fills with silence. The captain looks at my file, and I work to keep my knees still.

"I'm not done with you Sergeant Moses," Hurley says regaining his military bearing. "You better keep your nose clean because I'll be watching. You just get them colored musicians ready for next week's ceremony, and then on that train. After that, I don't want to hear another damn thing about you. You disgust me, and if you live through this war, you better get out of the army or I'll see to it that you do."

Hurley isn't going to bring me up on charges, but I also know he believes Pit's complaint. He scans the file for the last time, closes it and puts it in his side drawer. He dismisses me without looking up.

The captain's colored clerk stands when I enter the anteroom. "Good day, sergeant," he says, then adds: "take it easy."

"Is there any way to keep this quiet, corporal?" I ask.

"There will be no leaks from *this* office, but I can't speak for Private Turner."

I step down from the porch. All I want is to get away from the captain's office, and walk away my misery. A dozen yards up, I see Pit standing near the walkway.

"Now who's the nigger?" he snarls at me when I pass.

I stop in my tracks. The last twenty minutes of insult and indignity has made me a stick of dynamite with a burning fuse.

236

It is only because Pit wears the uniform, that I don't kill him on the spot.

"Private Turner," I say with the tone I used the first day I met him, "you're playing with fire."

I move quickly up the road, and am halfway to the band field when I look back and see him following me. We are the only two people on this secondary road leading to the outskirts of the base. I turn off the road onto a dirt path that leads to the water towers on the east side of the base. Pit soon catches up with me and I spin to face him.

"What do you want?"

"You know what I want, muthafucka."

I do know. Pit's rage is visible. He understands Hurley won't act on his complaint, so he wants his own justice. Five minutes ago, I would have easily accepted his challenge, and likely killed him. But my anger has turned to disappointment, in myself and the army.

"I don't want to fight you, Turner. You're risking your whole career. Use your head, boy."

Pit won't be appeased. His anger makes him reckless and he lunges at me, falling to his knees when I sidestep. He looks up, his eyes wild. He raises himself from the sand and lifts his fists.

"Fight me, you little sissy," he screams.

237

I know I will have to accommodate his fury so I take a fight stance. Pit is strong, taller than me and almost twenty years younger, but he is no match for my experience with man-to-man combat. We exchange punches toe-to-toe for several minutes and I let him hit me a few times. Once in the jaw with a solid right hook.

"I hate you," he says a few times out of breath, swinging wildly and missing.

"Have you had enough?" I ask, ducking his blow and counterpunching.

"I'll kill you," he says.

I believe I owe Pit this fight, but I don't want to hurt him so I am careful to hit him where it won't show, or do too much damage.

We are only a few yards off the secondary road, and I hear a vehicle approaching, so I punch Pit in the solar plexus, doubling him over, and put him in a choke hold until he blacks out. I am crouching low in the scrub bush while Pit lays unseen nearby, when the Jeep jerks up the road. It throws swirls of sand, stretching in all directions, into the dry air.

Chapter 36

(Boone)

It has already been a long journey—two days and one night. It started with a hot, two-hour bus trip to Fort Bragg in Fayetteville, where I boarded the first of two trains that would get me to Tucson, Arizona. The trip has not been boring. I've talked to the porters about train travel, and met lots of other soldiers.

I am on a train platform having a smoke during a brief stopover near Albuquerque, New Mexico when I see the engineer walking the length of the train...first down the yard side and then back up the passenger boarding side. He stops a few times shining a long-handled torchlight into the crevices of the train's underside. He pulls a small rag from the pocket of his striped coveralls, leans into the gap between each car then lifts himself into the space for a closer look. When he steps down to the platform, he tucks the rag and light into his coveralls and takes a small black notebook from his shirt pocket. I approach him.

"Those couplers must get a lot of metal fatigue."

The engineer looks at me curiously for a moment, but doesn't speak. He writes something in his notebook.

"I've been reading about metal fatigue in airplanes, and they have some kind of acid wash you can use to show the fracture lines in the metal."

The man stares at me this time.

"*You*, been reading about metal stress?" he asks.

"Yeah, I'm joining the Tuskegee Airmen next week as a mechanic."

He seems to recognize the name of the famous colored unit, and nods.

"At home, I just use coca cola. Once a month, I wipe down our truck and tractor chassis with it. The oil and dirt come right off and leaves little bubbles anywhere there's a small crack line. Over time, I keep an eye on the crack and sure enough, sooner or later, she'll become a problem."

"That's makes good sense, boy" he says without any attempt to insult. He opens the notebook again, and jots a couple of things. "Good luck to you."

Most of the colored soldiers I meet are impressed when I tell them I'm joining the airmen.

"You a Tuskegee Airman?" they ask enthusiastically while I try to explain I'll be a mechanic. "Hey, this boy's with the Airmen," they proclaim to anyone nearby and heads turn towards me and guys give me the thumbs-up, or flash the double V sign-the forefingers of one hand held up against the palm side of the other forefingers. It's clear to me that I carry the weight of my race with the Tuskegee assignment, and to tell the truth, I'm proud to do so.

It's just after two o'clock in the morning, and the train is scheduled for no more stops until well after dawn. One or two people are reading, but most passengers are sound asleep. Tomorrow, I'll arrive in Tucson and I can't relax enough to sleep, so I stand at the back of the compartment smoking a cigarette. A short, grey-haired porter, wearing his white jacket comes through the adjoining car and approaches me.

"Can't sleep, soldier?"

"No sir."

"You don't have to call me sir but I appreciate that someone has taught you to respect your elders."

I smile. "I have girl problems, that's why I can't sleep."

"Don't we all," he says returning the smile. He's already interested in the conversation to come.

I tell him the whole story. I surprise myself that I am willing to tell this stranger so much about my personal life, and by the time I'm done we have gone through two cigarettes a piece. It's against the rules for porters to smoke while on duty, but there is no one to see us at this hour of the night.

"Your Lil sounds like a special young lady. What you say about her reminds me of my own sweet wife, Rebecca. She passed away nearly six years ago now, but she was the love of my life, and we never once had a cross word between us."

241

Suddenly, I'm filled with anxiety. I don't know what I'll do if Georgette doesn't agree to marry me. I don't even know if she'll want to see me.

"When you get there, boy, you need to ask for the chaplain," the porter orders as if reading my mind.

"What?" I say shaking off sad thoughts.

"If you ask to see the chaplain, they'll let you in. Base chaplains spend most of their time counseling lonely, or hurt soldiers. Oh, they spend a few hours each week preparing and presenting their sermons, but the rest of the time they're more like mothers than army officers."

"So how does that help me?" I ask.

"When you get to the front gate, show them your orders to join the Airmen, and ask to speak to the chaplain for the colored soldiers. They'll have to call him to get permission for you to come in. When the chaplain asks what's your business, you tell them you're about to join the Tuskegee Airmen, and you have a message from home for Private First Class Lil... what's her last name?" He looks up at me to ask.

"Well, her name is actually Georgette Newton. Lillian is her middle name, so that's why I call her 'Lil'. He pauses to take in this information, then smiles.

"Right, I understand. I called my wife Reba."

"So, you tell them you have a message for PFC Newton, and it is a matter of urgency," he continues. "You have to use this Tuskegee thing man. It will open doors for you," he reminds me.

For the first time in a couple of days, I feel the sense of rightness I had when I began this trip. I will see Lil, and nothing will stop me. The porter, Mr. John Sherwood, and I shake hands, and he pats me on the back like a long-lost friend.

Chapter 37

(Sgt. Moses/Pit)

After the Jeep is out of view, I brush the sand from my
uniform, and check on Turner. He is still out cold, but breathing
normally. I should go back to duty, but I need to do some
thinking, and I need a drink.

At mid-morning the tavern is empty except for the civilian
staff preparing for evening. Only off-duty, or furloughed
soldiers will be here this time of day and, thankfully, I have the
place to myself. I sit at one of the booths away from the bar and
out of view of the door. I know the staff at the tavern and they
know me. In no time, one of them comes over.

"How're you doing this morning, sergeant?"

It's Grady one of the bartenders. He's spent many hours
listening to me complain about the brass, the Freedom Band, and
lazy-ass recruits. I'm sure he notices the bruise on my jaw.

"Not so good, Grady. I need a bourbon on the rocks."

He moves away to get my drink, no questions asked. If
anyone sees me drinking while I'm on duty I'll be in big trouble.
But shit, I'm already in trouble. I trace a deep scratch in the
table with my finger, and catch sight of my new ring. Bonnie
and I exchanged small, gold rings at the end of our vacation to
symbolize our commitment to each other.

I've always tried to hide my preference for men, but I haven't always been as discrete as I should. That's why the Fort Meyer situation got out of hand. It's only since I've been at Huachuca that I've really settled down, and I am truly content with the relationship I have with Bonnie.

Grady returns with my drink which he's disguised in a coffee mug— good old Grady. I don't dare stay here long. Captain Hurley has spies all around the base, and now that he has a particular interest in me, I'll have to watch my every move. But, I really need this drink, and after the first long sip, I feel my frayed nerves reconnect. I have only days before I'll be leaving this base, and I desperately need to bide my time and control my emotions. I've been through this before. This kind of rumor can be more persistent than others, because it's fueled by fear and curiosity.

I was very lucky not to be discharged at Ft. Meyer. The Commanding Officer got a call from one of the important, white businessmen in southwest Florida after I was discovered in a compromising position with his son. The son's sexual habits were known to his family, but they couldn't abide the idea of him being with a Negro. The C.O. at Fort Meyer had always been sympathetic to the challenges of the colored troops. Because he didn't want to spoil my otherwise exemplary record, he gave me a choice—a quiet transfer, or a very public discharge. I'd requested a transfer to Camp Benning to be nearer to Bonnie, but because of my success in training colored recruits, I was sent to Huachuca. Now my career was again in jeopardy.

I drain the rest of my drink, pop a stick of Juicy Fruit gum in my mouth and leave the tavern with a wave to Grady. This morning, Sgt. Terry had said he could get along without me at band practice, now his words make more sense to me. Huachuca is like a small town, and news travels fast. I know I'm about to have my most difficult week of my life.

When I open my eyes I am face down on the ground, and for a moment I think I've fallen asleep in one of the meadows near the orphanage. Then I realize it isn't soft grass next to my nose, but a scratchy desert shrub. I struggle to my knees and shake my head. I must have passed out. I push my fingers deep into the sand to steady myself and see my bloody, scraped knuckles. Then, I remember where I am, and pull myself upright to continue the fight. Sgt. Moses is nowhere in sight. The muthafucka has run away, and it also looks like he's beaten my ass.

I spot my cap a few feet away, pick it up, and stumble toward the road that leads to the parade field. Moses has another think coming if he believes this fight is over. My stomach and sides are sore, and my legs are unsteady, but I'm going to find him. I don't care what happens to me now. I'm through with this army shit. Nobody else plays by the rules, so why should I.

Behind me I hear someone calling my name. Sylvester is running toward me.

"Pit, I've been looking for you everywhere. You were supposed to report back to the work detail after you left Hurley's office. Sgt. Tyler sent me to find you."

"I don't need nobody looking for me, and Tyler can kiss my black ass."

"Man, what happened to you? There's sand all over your face."

I hadn't noticed the sand, and when I try to brush myself off, and tuck in my shirt, I realize it is torn. But, I'm not about to tell Sylvester that Sgt. Moses had whipped me.

"I was running and, uh saw a snake, and I must of fell down that hill back there, and hit my head on something. But, I'm alright now."

"Well, if you're okay, you better double time it back to the barracks, change clothes, and get on over to the excavation site. I'll tell Tyler what happened. Pit, he's seeing red."

I watch Sylvester go back the way he came, and I'm not sure I'll follow him. I don't care if Tyler is mad. He set me up. It was his idea to file a complaint against Sgt. Moses. I might not go back to the barracks at all. What's Tyler going to do to me, throw me in the brig? Give me hard labor? Shit, I feel like I'm in a damn prison already.

When I left Brickstone I was the oldest of the boys. It had been my home since I was five years old and I had to leave because I'd turned eighteen. The day I was to report to the army transport train, I told the orphanage kids and Miss Marsh not to worry about me because I was going to do a man's work in the army. I remember how they looked at me like I was some kind of hero. One boy even carried my suitcase to the road, and waited with me for the bus. I wonder what those kids would think if they saw me now.

I can't stay at Huachuca. The army isn't the place for me. If I'm not going to do the work of a soldier, I might as well cut out. But I still have unfinished business. I don't care what Captain Hurley says, Moses isn't going to get away with acting like a big man, when he's really something else.

Chapter 38

(LeRoy)

It is Wednesday evening and I'm in a long line at the rec center, but only a man away from one of the precious telephones. The timing will be just right to reach Mr. Giles at the church before choir rehearsal begins.

I know his routine. He will come home from school, make his mother a good dinner, and then walk to the church. He'll lay out the hymnals in the first two pews of the sanctuary and then practice on the organ for an hour before the choir members arrive. He'll be sure to answer the phone just in case it's his mother calling.

The guy ahead of me is talking to his girl and I keep a respectful distance so he won't think I'm listening, but he seems to want an audience because he turns to me and winks before he says: "I don't care what she said, you know I only love you." A minute later, he places the phone in the cradle and says to me: "Man, this war is really hard on my love life. When I was home I could keep my women away from each other, but now they're beginning to compare notes. You know what I mean?" he gives another wink.

The church phone rings six times before it's picked up.

"Absalom Baptist Church."

"Hello, Mr. Giles? This is LeRoy."

"What? Is this LeRoy Dowdell?" he shouts.

"Yes. I'm calling from the base. How are you sir?"

"I'm fine LeRoy, just fine. How are you, son?" He hesitates. "Is everything okay?" he continues to shout.

I tell Mr. Giles about the engagement gift I've bought Georgie and about the trip we've planned. I tell him I love her, and she loves me, and how I believe she is the only one around who understands me. Mr. Giles doesn't interrupt. He listens while I talk nonstop for a minute and a half.

"That all sounds good, LeRoy. This is an important time in your life and you're about to make some very important decisions. Now here's a question for you, son. Do you feel at peace with your choices?"

His question makes me catch my breath. I'm not at peace at all. So far the army, the Freedom Band, and even Georgie haven't taken away the sick, empty feeling I have in my chest. I can't talk about this with any of the guys...they would think I was crazy, and maybe I am.

"Are you still there, LeRoy? Is there some way I can help you?"

I know I have only a few more minutes of phone time. I lower my voice.

"Mr. Giles, I need to know if I'm making a mistake about Georgie. I need someone to tell me what to do."

"Be true to yourself son," he says as if that makes it clear.

Neither of us says a thing for a moment, until I remember that next week, I'll be on trains and boats far away from anyone I can confide in.

"Mr. Giles, I love Georgette, but I don't want to disappoint her."

"I understand, LeRoy," he says in his patient voice. The one he uses when he wants me to work out a problem for myself.

"There's something else. I don't know how to explain it."

There is the loud sound of static when neither of us is speaking. I lower my voice to a whisper.

"I'm different from the other guys, Mr. Giles."

"I know LeRoy."

"I'm not interested in the same things they are, and...I don't have the same feelings."

"I *know* LeRoy," he says again, but differently this time. He does understand.

"I need to ask you a question."

"Yes, LeRoy. You can ask me anything."

"Did you come to Arizona to see Sgt. Moses?"

"Yes. He's a close friend, and very dear to me," he says without hesitation.

"There have been some rumors here about the Sarge, and I think he's in trouble."

"Yes, he does have some trouble. He's told me, and I'm worried for him."

"If he's important to you, Mr. Giles, then I want to help him. But I don't know how."

"I'm not sure *what* we can do for him. There is not much understanding about men like us. People have a lot of fear about homosexuals, and that can lead to terrible acts."

I've only heard that word once or twice, but it stirs me. Some of the white guys in the band joke with each other about being 'homo'.

"LeRoy, you need to be careful. If you defend Robert, uh I mean Sgt. Moses, if you defend him too much, the men will begin to wonder about you. You don't want to jeopardize your opportunity to go to Europe. It's important for you to get there."

"Do you think I'm a homo...homosexual, Mr. Giles?" my hand is cupped over the mouthpiece of the phone.

"I don't know. What do you think?"

"But I love Georgie, how can I love her if I'm like..."

"Like me, LeRoy?"

I'm embarrassed. I hope I haven't insulted this man that I admire.

"LeRoy, some men can have the same feelings of love for a man, as they do for a woman. As human beings, God has made us in so many variations."

"Like *Variations on a Theme by Joseph Haydn*," I blurt out and then feel foolish. Mr. Giles laughs and finally, I do too.

"Yes. Just like that, LeRoy."

252

I was right to call him. We say our goodbyes, and I look at the man behind me who gives no indication he has overheard my conversation. I go outside to get some fresh air, and look up to the sky, deep black and filled with stars. The night is still, my mind is buzzing, like the phone wires on the high poles bleached white by the desert's sun.

Chapter 39

(Georgette/LeRoy)

"Yes, I'm excited, LeRoy and a little nervous too."

We are on a bench outside the recreation hall, sitting close but not daring to hold hands in this public part of the base. We have only a half-hour before we must return to our respective barracks, and I muster the courage to ask a question that has been on my mind for weeks.

"Have you ever been with a girl, LeRoy?"

He looks over at me. He's about to say something, then shoves his hands into his coat pockets.

"This is a big step for both of us," I say gently.

I can tell he's embarrassed, and I make sure no one sees me when I slip my hand in his pocket to rub his palm. He squeezes my hand tightly.

"I don't want you to be disappointed," he says.

"I won't be disappointed. We'll learn together. As long as we love each other, everything will be okay."

But, I'm not as confident as I pretend. Growing up on a farm, I've witnessed the mating of our animals and I've asked questions, but my parents always gave me answers that didn't satisfy my curiosity. What I know about sex between a man and a woman is what I've read about in romance magazines, or heard the girls talk about in the barracks long after the lights were turned out.

Both Clarice and Loretta have experience with men. Clarice has mentioned an affair with a man she knew in Alabama, but she won't talk much about it. Maybe I can get one of them to give me pointers.

"Did you tell Pit we're going away for the weekend?"

"I tried to tell him, but he doesn't care what I do anymore."

"I know. He's really changed. Sylvester thinks Pit and Sergeant Moses might have had a run in."

"What do you mean?"

"Sylvester says a couple of days ago Sgt. Tyler sent him after Pit, and when he found him, his shirt was torn and his knuckles were bruised. Sylvester knows more, so does Loretta, but they won't tell me what's going on."

"Georgie, I'm so glad I have you. Things are changing so fast with our other friends, and with the band. Don't you feel it?"

"I do feel it. We're being blown around in a whirlwind. Maybe it's the war…it makes everything urgent."

LeRoy is quiet, slouched on the bench, his hands still in his pockets, and his head down. So often, he reminds me of a lost little boy.

"Have you talked to your parents, Leroy?"

"No, not yet. But, I plan on calling mother before I leave base."

"Have you called your folks?" he asks.

"No, I didn't call at all last week, but I sent a letter. I'm afraid my mother might hear something in my voice."

"I did speak with Mr. Giles."

"Oh. Did you ask him about Sergeant Moses?"

"Yes. He said he's known him for a long time and they are dear friends."

"Friends?"

"More than friends."

There is so much about life and love I do not understand. There is simplicity in the happy endings of movies, and the smiling faces on each turn of the page in my magazines. I thought life away from the farm would be like that, exciting but easy. I've come to learn that a person's way of looking at life makes them who they are. I may see something as one way but another person will see the same thing very differently. It's not simple, but I think maybe it makes life more interesting.

"Georgie, you know that I love you," LeRoy says out of the blue.

"And I also love you," I reach for his hand again.

Suddenly, soldiers are swarming past our bench. I look at my watch. We have fifteen minutes to get to our barracks.

"So, I'll meet you at Kenny's on Friday, at eighteen hundred hours," LeRoy says.

"Okay, soldier," I look at him with all the love I feel. "I hope I can sleep tonight."

"I know what you mean," he says squeezing my arm.

I join a group of WAACS heading to our section of the camp and LeRoy trots off to the Freedom Band barracks.

I've thought a lot about my call with Mr. Giles. I don't blame him for being the way he is, he can't help it. But, it must be very hard for Sgt. Moses to be one way, and act another.

I'm not like them. I'm *not* a homosexual. The feelings I've had before were just something I was going through. I love Georgie, and when she and I make love this weekend, that will prove I'm a regular guy.

I arrive at the barracks with ten minutes to spare. Sgt. Moses is already taking the bed check, and he nods as I come through the door. The barracks are unwelcoming at night. The overhead lights cast a gloomy, minor chord feel. Guys are reading on their bunks, writing letters, shining their shoes or just doing nothing. Moses approaches my bunk as I make ready for bed. I spot a bruise on his cheek, and wonder if it is the result of a fight with Pit.

"Dowdell."

"Yes, Sarge. I know I'm a little late. Sorry."

"Tell me something about PFC Turner."

I'm surprised Moses has brought up Pit just when I was thinking about him, but I try to sound casual.

"What do you want to know about him Sarge?"

"Well, I know he's from some small town in Georgia. Does he have any family?"

"I don't think he has any family."

"Well what did he do before he joined the army?"

"Uh, I don't really know Sgt. Moses. Uh, I think maybe he did some farming."

"Damn it, Dowdell, can't you tell me anything about Turner? I thought the two of you were good friends."

"We used to be, but I don't see him much anymore with the band and all."

Sgt. Moses stares at me with a look of frustration. I try to think of something I can tell him about Pit.

"He was a hell of a ball player back home. A big man around town," I say.

"Why is he so angry?" Moses asks.

"He wasn't always angry. It's just that he used to feel important, and now he's not such a big deal anymore."

"Okay, Dowdell. That's all. Lights out in five."

Maybe what Sylvester told Georgie was right. Maybe the Sarge and Pit did have a run in, and from the looks of Moses, Pit may have gotten the better of him.

Chapter 40

(Boone/Georgette)

The train porter, was right. When I arrived at the gate at
Fort Huachuca in the late afternoon without an appointment, the
MPs eyed me suspiciously. But after I showed them orders to
report to the Tuskegee Airmen, they relaxed a bit and let me call
the chaplain's office. The chaplain's clerk came to the front gate
to fetch me, and escorted me to the Negro chapel.

"So you're going to be with the Airmen?" the clerk asks as
we walk to the rear of the base.

"Yes, I'm reporting next week to Michigan. I'll be a
mechanic."

"Well, the airmen are sure doing us proud."

The chapel is a simple building. Only the wood cross
trimmed in metal over the front door gives away its purpose.
The clerk leads me next door, to a small cottage.

"This is Chaplain Anderson's office, and personal quarters,"
he explains.

The chaplain is a tall, distinguished man with smooth,
brown facial skin that extends to a bald spot separating his neatly
trimmed side hair. His insignia is of a first lieutenant, but he
wears his shirt tie-less, and open at the collar. He probably
wouldn't get away with that casualness, if he had any other kind
of duty, but as a chaplain, his informal appearance must make

people feel more comfortable talking to him. I stand at attention and salute, and he returns the salute.

"What can I do for you today, Mr. Mack?" he asks sitting down in a wide chair covered in brown and white plaid fabric.

"Have a seat," he points to the brown leather settee across from him.

"Sir, I came here to see one of the WAACS on base, Private First Class, Georgette Newton. I have a message for her from home."

The chaplain studies me for a moment, then smiles. "Is the message from you?"

Chaplain Anderson has put two and two together rather quickly. I did the best I could to shave and clean up on the train, but I'm sure I look rumpled and tired after my long trip. I study my new army boots for a moment. I believe I should tell the absolute truth.

"Yes, sir, the message is from me. I want to ask her to marry me. I've known her all my life, sir. We grew up together in a small town in North Carolina. She's a wonderful girl, and I just have to know if she'll wait for me, before I leave for duty with the air squadron."

I say my piece in one breath and then, exhausted, lean back on the settee.

"Well Private Mack, that's quite a message you want to deliver. I take it PFC Newton, didn't know you were coming to see her, and that's why you've asked to see me?"

I nod a 'yes' to his question.

"You took quite a risk coming all this way from North Carolina, unexpected and uninvited."

"Yes sir, I know. It's the only thing I could think to do. I have to see her."

"What makes you think Private Newton will want to marry you?"

His question flings me into panic. I am crazy to have come.

"You're right, sir. I really don't know what she'll say." I put my elbows on my knees, and press my forehead into the palms of my hands for just a moment. Then I sit up straight. "But, I have to try."

"Of course you do," Chaplain Anderson agrees. "I know PFC Newton, she regularly attends our Sunday service. She seems like a spirited young woman, and a good Christian," he adds.

The chaplain and I talk for another twenty minutes then he stands up, and I follow suit.

"You wait here, Mr. Mack. I'll send for Miss Newton, and you'll have your chance to speak with her."

"I'm grateful, sir."

I accept the chaplain's offer of lemonade, then I lean back on the settee and inhale the first full breath of air I've taken in more than three days.

The phone rings at fifteen hundred hours in the personnel office. It's Clarice's turn to answer the phone.

"Chaplain Anderson wants to see you, Georgette," she looks worried.

When there is bad news from home, it is often the chaplain who delivers it.

"Did he say what he wanted?" I ask.

"His clerk only said you should report immediately."

I take a few minutes to arrange the folders on my desk so they can be re-filed in case I don't return right away. I'm rattled and I pray nothing is wrong with mama, daddy or my sisters. I take a deep breath, hurry my tasks, grab my Hobby and head for the door.

The personnel building is at the center of the base, near the hospital, and it will take ten minutes to walk to the chapel, so I decide to sign for one of the jeeps. Driving is another perk of being in the army. At home I occasionally drove the old truck around the farm, but that was just a little ride up an old dirt road to deliver lunch to the workers daddy hired for the tobacco crop. I would load the truck with baskets of thick pork sandwiches wrapped in brown paper, a bushel of apples, or a washtub of ice filled with sliced watermelon, add a couple of jugs of hot coffee and milk, then drive to the field. At Huachuca, my clerk duties require me to drive almost every day, picking up and delivering files throughout the base. It wasn't long before I could handle a Jeep without any trouble at all.

I arrive at the chaplain's office in just a few minutes and Chaplain Anderson's clerk greets me. "You have a visitor, Private Newton, but the chaplain wants to talk to you first." He points me to the chaplain's office while I wonder who this visitor might be.

The chaplain is at his desk, writing on a pad of light blue paper. I stand at attention. He calls 'at ease' and asks me to sit in the side chair. As is the protocol for WAACS, I remove my hat, and then wait as the chaplain continues his note using an elegant black fountain pen to execute a flowing cursive. The chaplain notices my anxious look and immediately stops writing, and presses a piece of thin white paper over the fresh writing to blot the ink.

"I'm sorry, Miss Newton," he says. "You must think I've called you here for bad news, and that is not the case."

I'm relieved and my shallow breathing quickly returns to normal. I have been wringing my cap in damp hands, and I smile at the chaplain and try to smooth the cap against my lap.

"I'm working on Sunday's sermon. Are you familiar with Philippians, Miss Newton?"

I certainly am familiar with that book of the New Testament. Mama is part of the team of women who teaches Sunday school, and we often sat with her on Saturday evenings as she read bible verses, and practiced her lessons on us. Furthermore, mama has more than once used Philippians to make points to me about my impatience and restlessness.

"Yes, sir, I do know it," I finally say.

The Chaplain looks at me and I think he wants me to say more.

"Paul is speaking to the Philippians about being more God-like by seeing the best in people, and to learn to be more content in their circumstances," I say.

"Well, yes, that is certainly part of what Paul is saying in his letter to the Philippians," the chaplain agrees. "But he also says in chapter 4, verses 6-7 that we should not be consumed by worry, that if we place our cares in God through prayer, he will give us peace."

I consider what Chaplain Anderson says. "I remember now, sir. Mama says it is a peace so deep that we can't even understand it, but when we have it, we know things will be alright. She says that's the peace she has about daddy and us kids."

"Your mother is a wise woman, Miss Newton. Mr. Mack is here to see you." The chaplain's words startle me. I think I've heard him wrong.

"What, sir?"

"PFC Mack is in my garden. He's come here to see you. He has a message for you, a message of home."

I stand up in shock. My knees are unsteady. The chaplain also stands.

"Boone is here?"

"He's in the garden. Come, I'll walk you back."

I follow the chaplain out the front of his cozy house, stepping on round, paving stones that circle to the back. The path is lined with beautiful shrubs and a few early spring blooms of lavender and orange on either sides of the walkway. He must give a great deal of time and water to these plants. I am wringing my hat again, then remember I am out of doors and should be wearing it. When we reach the garden there is a stone patio surrounded by a ring of cactus and other desert plants, some vibrant purple. There is a cross sculpture and two stone benches. It must be a beautiful place to watch the sunsets.

Boone sits on one of the benches, and stands when we enter the garden. He is handsome in his uniform and seems taller than the last time I saw him. The sun is nearly behind him and I can't see his face so well, but I see the white of his teeth grow and grow. He walks toward me. "I'll give you two a little time," the chaplain says, and retreats into a rear door of the house.

"Boone, what are you doing here?"

I am amazed he is at Fort Huachuca. He doesn't answer, he just leans down, and pulls me into his embrace, and I feel the strength of his arms and chest as he lifts me off my feet.

"Lil, I had to see you. I have so much to say to you. You got my letter?"

"I did get your letter."

I need to sit down so I pull away from him, and move to the closest bench. He sits next to me. He takes my hand, and I let him hold it.

"I can't stay long, I have to leave tomorrow, but I needed to see you. I love you, Lil."

"You should have told me you were coming."

"There was no time. You didn't call and... What's happened? Do you still love me?" His questions come fast.

I think of what the chaplain said about Philippians, and I also remember something mama always says, and then the answers become clear to me.

"Let's talk," I say to Boone.

Chapter 41

(LeRoy/Georgette)

I have a nervous stomach this morning, and instead of going to breakfast with the unit, I remain in the barracks. Since my talk with Mr. Giles, I've kept mostly to myself.

Several people have told me Pit is angry with me for not taking his side against Sgt. Moses. He's been drinking heavily, and talking about me behind my back. When Loretta tried to caution him about it, Pit told her to stay out of his business, and grabbed her arm so hard it caused a bruise.

The whole mess with Sergeant Moses is taking a toll on the Freedom Band. One of our guys overheard a white band member trashing Sarge and came to his defense. A fist fight broke out between the two, and then colored and white soldiers started shoving and pushing until Sergeant Terry broke it up. Although, some of the Negro band members are embarrassed by the Sarge, they understand what is skin deep trumps everything else in this white man's army.

Georgie and I are meeting at Kenny's tonight. We'll have a bite to eat before we catch the bus to Albuquerque. Another stomach cramp makes me grunt with pain, and I touch the pocket holding Georgie's engagement gift, and try to calm my nerves. When I get to town, I'll stop by the record store. Music always makes me right.

When I departed the chaplain's garden, my head was spinning. Boone is an understanding man and he listened very carefully as I explained my feelings to him. It was the hardest decision I've ever had to make. The chaplain was supportive of us both, and Boone and I held each other a long time before I left.

I arrive back at the personnel office after nearly two hours away, and Clarice and Loretta are eager to know why the chaplain has sent for me. Their mouths hang open when I inform them of Boone's surprise visit to the base.

"How did he look in his uniform? Loretta asks.

"Why didn't you bring him over to meet us?" Clarice adds.

"I couldn't bring him around, he wasn't even supposed to be on base, but he looked really good."

"What did you tell him about Leroy?" Clarice asks.

"Look, I better get back to work, and I have to visit the toilet first. I'll tell you all about it, later."

Loretta seems satisfied for the moment, but not Clarice. She follows me into the latrine.

"Well, what is it?" I ask her.

"You know LeRoy is going to ask you to wait for him tonight."

"Yes, I think he is," I admit.

I don't want Clarice to press me for more information and she doesn't, but she waits to see if I have more to say.

"Is Pit still spreading rumors about Sgt. Moses?" I change the subject.

"Yes, even more than before, and he's saying any soldier who takes Moses' side is not a real man either…like LeRoy."

Clarice has managed to bring the subject back around to her main area of interest.

"Clarice, the chaplain and I talked about the book of Philippians. He said it speaks of a 'knowing' that gives you great peace. But, you know what else it speaks of, the future…looking at what lies ahead, and not at what's behind us."

"So?" Clarice posed.

"So, I'm not going to be controlled by the past, I'm looking forward."

"I don't know what that means, Georgette," Clarice says shaking her head. Without a doubt Clarice has the best stare on the entire base. But, I won't say anymore, so she wishes me good luck and leaves the latrine.

I think about what Clarice has told me about Pit. He is turning on LeRoy. I was afraid that might happen. He's finally showing his true colors. Pit seemed like a good guy at first, with that easy smile and eagerness to have fun, but now I know beneath all that jiving he is a spiteful man. Still, I won't judge

Pit, just as I won't judge Sgt. Moses. I don't know what either of them has gone through in their lives.

LeRoy has always had music to make up for the things he couldn't find at home. I know I've been lucky. I grew up with a mother and father who cared about me, and the certainty of their love gave me the space to dream. Maybe Pit and the Sarge just never had a safe place to dream.

I quickly finish up my work, then go to the barracks to make the final preparations for my furlough. My base spies tell me LeRoy has already left for town. I imagine him at the small music store rummaging through sheet music, and talking to the clerk about the latest Cab Calloway record until it's time for our rendezvous at Kenny's. I check that my stocking seams are straight in the mirror, grab my coat and handbag and head for the door. The bus will be leaving for town in a half hour and I'm filled with anxiety and anticipation. I'm beginning a new phase of my life, and the searching is over.

Chapter 42

(Sgt. Moses)

Hurley's clerk, Corporal Anthony Wyatt, ignores the campaign to ostracize me and walks over to my table in the corner of the tavern. Several people take note. I don't care, because I am off duty, and on my third drink.

"Sergeant Moses, how are you doing?"

"Well, how do you think I'm doing corporal? People don't want to be around me, I hate my assignment, and this liquor is watered down."

The corporal takes in my self-pity then sits down.

"You must have something official to tell me if you're talking to me, Wyatt.

"Just some news I thought you should hear before everyone else does, sergeant. Rather than clamming up as he has been ordered, PFC Turner has continued his verbal attacks against you, and has convinced others in his unit to join him in the smear campaign.   But that's not the end of it. He's now also publicly criticizing the Freedom Band."

"He's just making matters worse," I say shaking my head.

"It's already worse. Captain Hurley has drawn up papers putting Turner on report, rescinding the leaves of everyone in his unit, and demoting Sergeant Tyler for his inability to keep his men under control. I thought you'd want to know since it's your old unit."

"Corporal, I'll be off the base, and out of the country in five days. Is there anything you can do to get Hurley to back down from this?"

The Corporal looks around to see who is watching. Several people are, so he lowers his voice.

"Look Sergeant Moses, Hurley is regular army. The rest of us are going home after the war, but he wants to make a career out of this shit." Wyatt pauses when he remembers that I, too, am a career soldier. "No offense meant."

I wave off the comment. I didn't know why he is being so frank, but I'm grateful to him, and he continues.

"Hurley can't afford to have the Freedom Band fail, and he doesn't want any negative reports about his division, he just wants all this to go away. If Turner had just kept his mouth shut, that would have been the case. But, with the rumors persisting, Hurley has received a couple of calls from headquarters. He's still playing off the problem as just the work of a disgruntled enlisted man, and the lack of discipline among the colored troops," the corporal explains.

"So if he gets rid of me and Pit, he gets rid of his problems."

"Right. As soon as we can find Turner, he's going to the stockade."

"What do you mean, when you find him?"

"Right now he's AWOL."

"AWOL," I am immediately sober. "That stupid...," I stop myself from calling him nigger. My use of that word on the first day I met Pit, might have been the start of all this trouble.

"His detail was doing excavation near the southeast fence line," Wyatt explains. "But when they finished for the day, he was missing."

I ask Wyatt to do what he can for Turner, and thank him for trying to help me, then it occurs to me I should ask why he has.

"Some of us aren't against you, Sgt. Moses. Some of us..." he folds his hands atop the table, "understand just what you're going through. You know?"

So, that's the reason Wyatt was so sympathetic in the captain's office, and that's why he is risking his reputation now. Blood is thicker than water, and those of us in 'the life' have a blood bond.

"I didn't know about you, corporal. I've been on the straight and narrow since I came to Huachuca," I confide.

"I know. *We* know. We'd already heard about you at Fort Meyer."

"Are there many of us at Huachuca?"

"More than you would ever suspect—colored, and white. But we are extremely careful."

I'm stunned that Wyatt knows of white homosexuals on the base. Things must really be changing as draftees from big cities

274

come into the army with more liberal attitudes about race and everything else.

"I think I better go now," Corporal Wyatt says rising from the table. "Hurley will want an update on the search for Turner. I'll do what I can to help him see the benefit of playing the situation low key."

Wyatt hesitates before leaving,

"Sgt. Moses, I want you to know a lot of the Negro officers and non-coms really respect what you've done to show the army that colored soldiers deserve to be in the action. It's too bad this thing had to come up now."

It will be dark in a few hours, and I'm free until it's time to tuck the colored band members into bed. So, I decide to look for Turner myself. Maybe, I can keep him from ruining his young life.

"I'm driving to the southeast quadrant to see how the new construction work is going," I say to the clerk in the transportation hangar. She is a WAAC in her late twenties, a white woman from Chicago. She and I have spoken before of the things we love most about our hometown.

"I guess you miss the training work, huh Sgt. Moses?" the clerk asks as she pencils in the form for me to sign out a Jeep.

"Yes, I miss it. The band detail isn't exactly what I thought I'd be doing during wartime."

"You've been in the service a long time, haven't you?" she asks.

"Yep. Twenty years. A long time."

"Well, it's a different army now, sergeant. Just look at me. Two years ago, who would have believed I'd be wearing a uniform?"

"You're right, Private Kinney. But, for some of us it's not changing fast enough."

The jeep bounces on the rocky, unpaved road that leads to the desolate southeast side of the base. As I expected, the Military Police are swarming the area looking for Turner. I signal to two MPs I know.

"Any sign of Turner yet?" I ask the colored driver.

"No. Not yet. The fence line is secure, so we don't think he could be in the desert. Nobody could jump over that fence."

He's probably right. The chain fence surrounding Fort Huachuca is ten feet high, and topped with barbed wire. But, Turner is strong and agile, and might have found a way over.

"Well, I'm going to take a look around the excavation site. I'll let you know if I see anything,"

"We've already been over there, but you're welcome to look. Hey, I thought you were assigned to that new band, Sarge. Why the interest?"

"Turner used to be one of my guys. He and I have had our issues, but I'm worried about him."

The two MPs exchange a glance. They have likely heard Turner's rants against me.

"Anyway, I feel kind of responsible for him running off. Maybe if I can talk to him, he might turn himself in. I'd hate to see him get a dishonorable. He could be a great soldier if we could get him to the front. He's raring to fight."

"Okay Sarge. But, if you spot him, let us know right away."

I hug the fence line, occasionally slowing the Jeep to look for places where Turner might have found a way over. The night wind is beginning to stir, distorting the fresh tire tracks of the MP vehicles. I am nearing the area where months ago, Turner, Dowdell and the others had the fight with the white soldiers. I turn off the Jeep engine, and walk to the edge of the construction site. The only sound I hear is the pelting of sand against the stacks of tin sheets on the ground. The digging is mostly completed, and large pieces of lumber fortify the hole until concrete can be poured.

The sky is dimming quickly, so I keep my eyes on the ground to avoid tripping over debris. Three yards away I see buckets and other tools piled together, a shovel handle sticks out from under a tarp that partially covers the mound. Two cinder blocks have been placed at the edge of the tarp to hold it down. I push at the closest block with my boot to make sure a scorpion hasn't made it a nesting place, then lift the block and throw it off to the side. As I do the wind lifts the corner of the tarp revealing PFC Turner. His face is crusted with dried blood and sand. His eyes are fixed in a wide death stare, and fire ants are already making a feast of him.

Chapter 43

(Georgette)

When I arrive at Kenny's, Leroy is waiting at a table near the back wall. He stands as I approach, and I can't help but smile at his striking good looks. His wide set eyes, smooth skin and dark, wavy hair shine in the harsh light of the restaurant.

Several of the women lounging at the counter, spin on their red stools to stare enviously when LeRoy kisses me on the cheek and holds out a chair for me to sit. His valise is on the chair next to him, and I put my coat, shoulder bag and a small travel bag on the other chair.

"Hi sugar," he says in his sweet baritone.

"Hi yourself, soldier" I reply nervously.

"So shall we order some food? We have an hour-and-a-half before we have to catch our bus,"

"I know, but we have things to talk about," I remind him, and he nods his agreement.

"I have something important to ask you, Georgie, but let's order our drinks first,"

We make small talk while we wait for the drinks to be served. LeRoy shows me the sheet music he's bought, and speaks excitedly about the new record he's heard by Louis Jordan. He is always passionate when he talks about music.

Our drinks arrive—a beer for me, and a scotch and water for LeRoy. I never had a drink at home, except for a sip of homemade wine I sneaked one Christmas when a relative brought it to our house. But since joining the army, I've learned to appreciate a cold beer. Once you got used to the bitterness, it could really give you a nice feeling.

LeRoy takes a not-so-short drink from his glass, and reaches into his pocket. He places a square white box with a pink bow on the table.

"Georgie, this is for you," he slides the gift across the table to me. "Open it," he says.

I look at it for a moment then slip the ribbon from the box and open the top. I fold back soft, white tissue paper to reveal a beautiful gold locket. The face of the locket is mother-of-pearl, with soft swirls of pink and blue, and just a hint of pale yellow. It hangs on a pink sash with a clip pin.

"It's lovely, LeRoy" I admit.

"Look inside," he urges.

I use my thumbnail to pry open the gold edge of the locket, and find a tiny photo of LeRoy in his band jacket. In it, he is smiling broadly, and looking proud and happy.

"It's an engagement gift, Georgie. I want to marry you when I get back from Europe. I love you, and want you for my wife."

I feel the tears form at the corners of my eyes, and I have to wipe them away before I can see his face clearly. He has more to say.

"We can move wherever you want, and have the kind of life we've talked about. We'll have lots of friends and go to parties and the symphony. We can even..."

"I can't marry you LeRoy. I'm sorry...I, I wanted to tell you face to face. I really care about you, but...but I'm in love with Boone, the boy from home."

LeRoy stares at me for a moment, then down at his hands on the table but says nothing. He is very still, and I wonder if this is the quiet before the storm. He reaches for his glass and drinks the rest of the scotch without stopping. After an agonizing minute, where I feel like bolting from the table, he has something to say.

"Why didn't you tell me before? We planned this trip, and you said you loved me, too." His voice is low.

"I'm sorry. I didn't realize the truth about things until today. Boone came to the base this afternoon, to ask me to marry *him*. I've known him all my life, LeRoy. He needs me, and he'll take care of me." Tears cloud my vision again.

"I don't blame you, Georgie. I wasn't sure if I could make you happy, and it's important to me that you be happy."

He looks at me a moment, then leans across the table. With his thumb, he wipes the tears from both my cheeks then puts the tip of his thumb into his mouth. "Scotch and tears," he says. "I think I'll write a sad song and call it that."

We sit quietly for another minute. I recognize the tune on the jukebox. It is by Billie Holliday. I feel a wave of relief, followed by guilt, but I'm not sure what to say. Then the words just come to me.

"LeRoy, you have the greatest gift. You encourage people with your music, and I know as long as you honor your talent, you'll have all the happiness you want."

He smiles, and I reach for my coat. "I have to go."

"You can't stay and at least have dinner?"

"No, no I can't."

I see a pained look in his eyes, then he ducks his head the way my father used to do when he was embarrassed.

"Please take the locket, Georgie. I want you to have it. I want to remember that you have it."

I don't think it's a good idea, but I can't refuse him anything else, so I put the box into my handbag. When I get to the door I look back, and LeRoy blows a kiss.

The air is cold now, and I button my coat all the way to the top. I'm going to meet Boone at the boarding house a few blocks away. Tomorrow, the east-bound train will take him home to say goodbye to his folks before he joins the Tuskegee unit. I'll ride with him as far as San Antonio, then return to

Huachuca. But, tonight we will sleep together for the first time. And it will be as man and wife.

Our marriage took place this afternoon in the beautiful garden behind the chaplain's house. Chaplain Anderson included Philippians in the simple, informal ceremony: 'Whatsoever things are honest, whatsoever things are just, whatsoever things are pure...if there be any virtue or any praise, think on these things,' he had read.

It is a fitting promise to make on your wedding day.

Chapter 44

(Sgt. Moses/LeRoy)

The morning air is brisk, the sky clear and the Huachuca
Mountains glow regally in the distance. Although unforgiving,
the desert can be a beautiful place. This afternoon I'll deploy
with the Freedom Band to begin a goodwill tour, but as soon as
the war is over I'm leaving the army, and moving to Atlanta to
be closer to Bonnie.

Turner's body also ships out today, back to Georgia in a
body bag. All the forms have been processed and the
investigation into his suspicious death is completed. I was the
primary suspect, until MPs found a dog tag concealed in the
construction debris. Two, new recruits finally admitted to
beating Turner to death and according to them, Pit started the
fight. They testified they were surveying the excavation as
ordered, when Turner spotted them and began cursing. "Why
ain't you honkies digging holes like me?" he'd screamed. Turner
was said to have charged at the recruits with a pick axe. We'll
never know the whole story, but the final report labeled PFC
Turner unfit for duty, and concluded his death was an accident.

"You can't blame yourself for what happened to that young
man, Robert," Bonnie tried to comfort me over the phone.

"But, I do blame myself. I was too hard on him. Maybe I should have recognized his foolishness was just a way to get attention in a place where he felt invisible."

"This war made us all hope things might change for the Negro," Bonnie said. "But nothing's really changed. We all have to be able to sacrifice a part of ourselves to fit in. Private Turner probably wasn't mature enough to understand that."

Bonnie's words stayed with me, but I was still distressed and took PFC Dowdell aside to talk about Turner.

"He was afraid of you, Sarge," Dowdell said nervously. "He'd never admit it, but I think he really looked up to you."

"Looked up to me?"

"He didn't have any family, and I think he wanted to become a real soldier, like you."

"I don't understand."

"He wanted to prove himself to you, and earn your respect, but you kept riding him and, uh, embarrassing him. So, well, when he heard about...you know."

"Go on Dowdell."

"Well, I think he was mad at himself for ever wanting to be like you."

"Private, it might not be obvious to you, but I was trying to help your friend Pit."

Dowdell shook his head. "All I know Sarge, is he wanted to be a hero like he was at home, and nobody would let him."

Not even me, I admit now to myself.

True to form, Hurley called Turner's murder an isolated incident that didn't suggest a race problem at Fort Huachuca. So with Turner dead, me leaving, and the Freedom Band about to give its first and last symbolic performance on base—it must be a good day for the captain.

I scan the band formation, and spot LeRoy. He looks snappy in his band uniform. All the men do. This Freedom Band thing might be just a public relations stunt, but the entire base has turned out for the farewell ceremony.

I've promised Bonnie I'll continue to watch out for Dowdell as we travel. I understand his girl has broken up with him, but he must be handling it okay, because he seems content when he is playing with the band. It will be his saving grace. Still, I'll keep an eye on him. And, for a little while longer, the brass will keep an eye on me.

Butterflies circle my stomach as we wait for the start of the parade. It will be a performance for the officers at Fort Huachuca, some military brass from Washington, DC, a congressman, and other local dignitaries. The All-American Freedom Band is a big deal, and there are times it seems more like we're readying for a war campaign than a band tour. In the last four days we've spent every waking moment preparing for our trip, and for this grand parade.

Captain Hurley has watched us practice for hours and appears as anxious as we are. Band Director, Bergen has a staff of six men who have made things ready. Band equipment and a trunk filled with music arrangements is already packed. Travel papers have been prepared for fifty-six band members, a four-member color guard, and Sergeants Moses and Terry. We received our new parade uniforms a few days ago, and they are beautiful. I've polished the brass buttons on my band jacket, the way I used to polish my rifle. We wear the new uniforms this morning and our shoes, instruments and equipment gleam in the sun. When we finish this performance we'll double time it to the barracks, pack our gear, change into travel clothes, and then meet the buses waiting to take us to a troop train.

The VIPs have arrived, and the review stands are filled with locals from town, and civilians who volunteer on the base. A lot of the colored troops stand along the parade line for a glimpse of the band, and to wish us well. The colored band members know we'll be representing our families, friends and the other Negro troops as we travel the world and entertain our soldiers on the front lines.

I think of my mother and father and wish they could see me now. I know Georgie, Clarice and Loretta are somewhere in the crowd. They've taken Pit's death very hard, especially Loretta.

Yesterday, Georgie gave me a picture of our old gang to take on the trip, and she offered me a peck on the cheek. She looked good, and seems very happy. Clarice also made a point of coming to see me.

"I just wanted to make sure you are doing okay, LeRoy,"

"To tell you the truth, Clarice. I'm glad to be leaving Huachuca tomorrow. This place holds a lot of bad memories for me."

"But, all the memories aren't bad, are they?"

"Well, no, not really. I'll always wish Georgie the best. She's lucky to have you for a friend, Clarice, and I'm glad we're friends, too."

"LeRoy, I want you to know that you can write me if you want, and I'll be sure to write back."

"I'm not much for writing, but I'd like to receive your letters, and I'll try to send you a postcard."

Clarice kissed me gently on the lips, and held me tightly around my waist, and I held her too.

The only sadness I feel today is for Pit. He was the first friend I made in the army, and there were many things about him that I admired. I wish I'd had a chance to tell him so before he died laying in one of those holes he hated digging.

Lieutenant Bergen raises his arms in the ready command, and I blink back tears. My stomach is fluttering with excitement, and I have to keep licking my lips so they won't be dry. When Bergen is sure every musician is set, he punches the air with his baton. The center snare drum marks our cadence, and the rest of the drums follow. Also on cue, the fluttering in my stomach ends and I feel the blood coursing through my veins. The crowd silences in anticipation of the music, and I raise the horn to my lips.

Epilogue
October 2004

(Georgette)

It is my 82nd birthday. I sit in the antique oak chair at the head of my dining room table which is piled high with torn wrapping paper and ribbons from my party gifts.

An hour before, the table held the bounty of a half dozen creative, southern cooks. There were three choices of meat: roast turkey, pork loin and meat loaf—all served with gravy. Ruthie made her sweet potato casserole topped with tiny roasted marshmallows, and her daughter, Carol, had baked dozens and dozens of braided rolls brushed with butter. Helen's collard greens, and fresh green beans were delicious, and other side dishes included sweet corn on the cob, Waldorf salad and a pineapple gelatin mold. For dessert, Barbara brought her signature banana cream pudding, based on mama's recipe. Also in my honor, was a big sheet cake with the number "82" written in blue icing, and circled by candles.

I basked in the attention of my family when they sang Stevie Wonder's version of the happy birthday song, and then passed around paper plates loaded with a square of yellow cake and a scoop of vanilla ice cream—my favorites. In all, fifteen adults and kids were gathered to celebrate with me. I look again at my gifts—a box of white handkerchiefs, a yellow sweater, three audio books, a rocking chair, tied with a big red bow, and a Groucho Marx nose given to me by my grandnephew, Nathaniel. He watched raptly when I opened his gift, and gave a long, belly laugh when I replaced my bifocals with the plastic glasses that held the bulbous nose and black mustache in place.

Now my sisters' husbands, and some of my nephews are clustered in front of the television watching a football game. The smaller kids are in the back yard swinging on the tire Boone hung from the big oak, and the women sit with me in the dining room, quietly talking about the men and kids. After a few minutes, I excuse myself to go to my front porch where I try out my new rocking chair. I want to be with my own thoughts.

Linda follows a few minutes later. She is my seventeen-year-old great niece, and my favorite because she reminds me of me.

"Do you need anything, Aunt Lil?"

"No Lindy, thank you for asking. I was just letting my mind travel back."

"Are you thinking about Uncle Boone?"

Actually, I *was* thinking about Boone, as I often do during these family times. Following the war, Boone and I returned home to Pender County where we lived for fifteen years. After both his parents had died, he sold the farm to his cousin, and we moved here to Washington, DC. It took Boone some time to adjust to city life, but once he found work as a mechanic at one of the airlines, he began to settle down real nicely.

I worked for twenty-eight years at the airport helping travelers with their lost bags and transporting passengers through the terminals. It was a good job, and I met lots of interesting people. Since Boone and I never had kids, we traveled all around the country during our vacations; and while mama and daddy were alive, we went back to Pender each year. Eventually, every one of my sisters followed me to DC. Boone died of a heart attack five years ago. We had our ups and downs like any married couple, but we had a full and happy life together.

"Yes," I finally say. "I *was* thinking about your uncle just now. Did I ever tell you that I almost didn't marry him?"

Linda's eyes grow very wide and I launch into my story. I tell her of my restlessness at home, and desire for adventures when I was just a little older than her. I talk about my try at teacher's college, and of my two years in the army with Clarice and Loretta. I also tell her all about LeRoy—his love of music, his proposal of marriage, and his travel to Europe with the Freedom Band.

It gets chilly on the porch, so we move inside to my bedroom, and I show her a photograph of me in my uniform and another one of me with my army buddies. These photos are displayed on my dresser next to the picture of Boone and me on our silver wedding anniversary. I pick up a small, carved wood box from the dresser, and sit on the edge of the bed. A slide at the bottom of the box reveals a hidden compartment, and I pull from it a gold locket with a mother-of-pearl face.

"Oh, this is so pretty, Aunt Lil."

"Look inside," I say.

Linda opens the locket and looks at the picture of a young soldier. He has a wide smile, and a twinkle in his eye.

"Is this LeRoy?" she asks excitedly.

I nod.

"Oh, he's very handsome, Aunt Lil."

"Yes, he was a good-looking boy...and a dreamer like you and me."

"Did he become a famous musician like he wanted?"

"Sort of," I say.

I'd lost track of most of the army gang, but Clarice and I have remained dear friends through the years, and it is she who has kept me updated on our old friends and acquaintances from Fort Huachuca. After the war, LeRoy and Clarice married and settled in Detroit. So, I tell Linda what Clarice told me.

"LeRoy stayed with the Freedom Band for the rest of his tour of duty, and after the army he played in several jazz bands, and he got to travel all over the world."

"Aunt Lil?" Linda hesitates to ask her question, and I don't rush her. I pick up the framed army portrait, and stare at the restless young girl I once was.

"Do you ever wish you'd married LeRoy instead of Uncle Boone, so you could have some of the adventures you wanted?"

It's not a question I mind. I've even asked it of myself a few times during a lifetime of marriage.

"I've had my full share of adventures, honey. Your uncle and I visited almost every state in the union, I got to live in a big city, and meet wonderful people, and I even managed to drag your uncle to a few dances."

"I can't imagine Uncle Boone dancing," Linda says shaking her head, and we share a chuckle.

"LeRoy and I would not have been happy together for long. Your uncle was able to give me his whole self. He understood who he was, and what he wanted."

"What do you mean, Aunt Lil?"

"It's a long story, dear, one we'll save for another time, but I'll tell you this, when LeRoy and I met, he was still in search of himself, and so was I."

Linda and I rejoin the family. Nathaniel is wrestling on the floor with one of his cousins. Barbara, Helen and Ruth are laughing and supervising their daughters in the kitchen cleanup. Some of the nieces and nephews are sitting on the floor playing a lively game of 'Go Fish', and the men have found another football game.

Linda goes to the kitchen and I put on my new yellow sweater and return to the porch. There are things I didn't share with Linda. It's true that Clarice had the life with LeRoy I'd wanted, but there were other things. Clarice recounted a time many years after the war, when she and LeRoy were together in Europe, where he was performing in a small Parisian club with a jazz quintet. LeRoy's teacher, Mr. Giles, and Sgt. Moses were living together in Spain at the time, and LeRoy invited them to Paris to see him play. Clarice said she watched LeRoy interact with the two, older men and his other friends, and knew then what she suspected was true. LeRoy loved her, but sometimes he kept the company of men. Clarice said it was a common thing among his circle of musician friends, and over time she and LeRoy worked out an understanding about it.

Clarice always knew how to be content in her circumstances, that is her genius. She and LeRoy live in Atlanta now, and I think I'll give her a call tomorrow.

The war brought us together—LeRoy, Sgt. Moses, Pit, Clarice, Loretta, me and all the others. We came to Fort Huachuca on different journeys, and some of us found just what we needed. It would take many subsequent years, and other wars for America's black soldiers to finally receive their full regard in this country. As human beings, we still have a long way to go when it comes to accepting people who are not like us. But, from what I've seen all these years, none of us is that different, one from another.

I lean back in my rocker, and listen to the happy sounds of family. I count myself very lucky for my own journey. I try to remember the phrase mama used to say. What was it? I smooth the wrinkles in my dress as I concentrate to recall, then I do. "Sometimes the long way round, is the shortest way home."

*****

About the Author

Cheryl Head is a Washingtonian (DC) resident, originally from Detroit. Head has communications degrees from Ohio University (M.A.), and Wayne State University (B.A.). She had a long career in public broadcasting at the local and national levels before turning to fiction writing. Head's travels have taken her to every continent except Antarctica and Australia, where she has researched the historical context of race and its intersectionality with current societal issues.

Head is the author of the award-winning, Charlie Mack Motown Mysteries. *Bury Me When I'm Dead*-is a Lambda Literary Award finalist. The series is included in the Detroit Public Library's African American Books list. *Long Way Home: A World War II Novel* was shortlisted for the 2015 Next Generation Indie Book Awards for African-American literature, and Historical Fiction.

Head is currently writing a novel on the historical practice of police brutality against the black community and its connection to the contemporary Black Lives Matter movement

Artist's Statement:
Much of what I write focuses on the themes of diversity (in its broadest sense), acculturation and tolerance, sometimes with a

bit of danger and always with a lot of humor, food and music.
I'm an ardent observer and listener, always trying to connect the
dots, which connect us to each other.

Made in United States
North Haven, CT
02 April 2023

34943444R00166